ENDANGERED
PEOPLES

By Karen Liptak

AN IMPACT BOOK
FRANKLIN WATTS
NEW YORK · CHICAGO · LONDON · TORONTO · SYDNEY

Photographs copyright © : Wolfgang Kaehler Photography: pp. 2, 112, 119, 126; AP/Wide World Photos: pp. 14, 23 bottom, 31 bottom, 38, 46 bottom; Gamma-Liaison: pp. 17. (G. Humer), 68 (Wendy Stone), 71 (K. Arkell); Impact Visuals: pp. 18, 31 top (both Milton Guran), 54 (Afrapix/Paul Weinberg); Anthro-Photo: pp. 23 top (Napoleon Chagnon), 36, 43, 103 (all I. Devore), 46 top (M. Shostak), 65, 66 (both Ed Tronick); Photo Researchers Inc.: pp. 62 (Christa Armstrong), 82 (H. Kanus), 85 (Ewing Krainin), 94 (Omikron); Archive Photos: pp. 84, 91; UPI/Bettmann Newsphotos: p. 89; The Bettmann Archive: p. 107; Alaska State Library, Historical Photograph Collections: pp. 110 top, 115 (B. B. Dobbs); Hudson's Bay Company Archives, Provincial Archives of Manitoba: pp. 110 bottom, 117.

Library of Congress Cataloging-in-Publication Data

Liptak, Karen.
Endangered peoples / by Karen Liptak.
p. cm.—(An Impact book)
Includes bibliographical references and index.
Summary: Examines five ethnic groups living tribal existences around the world and shows how assimilation into mainstream society and other factors are threatening their cultures.
ISBN 0-531-10987-9
1. Indigenous peoples—Juvenile literature. 2. Ethnology—Juvenile literature. [1. Indigenous peoples. 2. Ethnology.]
I. Title.
GN380.L56   1993
306'.08—dc20   92-41391   CIP   AC

Copyright © 1993 by Karen Liptak
All rights reserved
Printed in the United States of America
5 4 3 2

CONTENTS

INTRODUCTION   7

YANOMAMI OF THE AMAZON RAIN FOREST   13

SAN (BUSHMEN) OF THE KALAHARI DESERT   34

BAMBUTI (PYGMIES) OF THE ITURI FOREST   59

ABORIGINES OF AUSTRALIA   80

INUITS (ESKIMOS) OF THE ARCTIC   105

MOVING ON   138

ORGANIZATIONS OF INTEREST   144

SOURCE NOTES   147

GLOSSARY   149

BIBLIOGRAPHY   151

FOR FURTHER READING   155

INDEX   158

INTRODUCTION

Although the media often focus on the plight of endangered animals such as the jaguar, the humpback whale, and the green sea turtle, we seldom hear about people being endangered. Yet many groups living tribal existences are currently threatened with extinction. Often this involves a cultural extinction. A group's centuries-old customs are ignored and its everyday life-style is drastically changed. As people try to assimilate into mainstream society, or are forced to do so, many times they find themselves giving up the lifeways that made them unique. They continue to exist, yet an important part of their lives is missing. Sometimes the extinction is physical as well, as members of the group are killed, either directly or indirectly.

Their existence is jeopardized today for a variety of reasons that stem from the desires of intruders for their land. These outsiders are many and include farmers, miners, cattle ranchers, sheep herders, and government officials who want more land for everything from roads and hydroelectric power plants to dams and wildlife preserves.

Regardless of what force displaces them, the result is often the same. The tribal group, once lords of their land, become dispossessed, and when their life-style is interrupted, a whole range of problems befall them. These include joblessness, poor health, and limited educational opportunities. Their spirit, too, is dealt a heavy blow.

Today, as in the past, tribal people face great conflicts, both internal and external, once they are "discovered" by the outside world. Note that the word *discovered* is somewhat ironic, since tribal people have always been known to themselves and each other.

The pattern has been repeated many times. Tribal people, usually indigenous (native) to their land, enjoy a relatively simple life in which they are spiritually bound to their homeland. Many are hunters and gatherers whose survival skills enable them to reap the natural bounty of their land season by season. Their lives depend upon their intimate knowledge of their environment and their abilities to cooperate with each other.

Many of these tribes have been known about for centuries. Others have only recently been brought to the world's attention. It wasn't until 1930 that some 1 million tribal people who still live as our ancestors did in the Stone Age were discovered in the highlands of Papua New Guinea, located in the Pacific Ocean north of Australia. There, as in South America, previously uncontacted people are still being "found" by outsiders today.

Outsiders come, perhaps seeking fertile land, mineral riches, or a passage to another part of the world. Often, explorers and adventurers arrive first, bearing items to trade for tribal goods. Unfortunately, even with good intentions, they usually bring diseases to which the natives have no resistance.

Many tribal people have died as a result of epidemics of deadly "imported" diseases such as measles, malaria, smallpox, and influenza. Add to that the missionaries who, in their zeal to convert natives to Christianity, have caused serious breaches in tribal life. Tribal children are sent away to missionary or government schools, where their own culture and language are not taught. This is often the result of misguided policies intended to help natives assimilate into mainstream society. The result is that children return home to find that they are strangers to their parents' time-honored ways. Often they cannot even speak the same language. Forced assimilation has created so many problems for tribal people that in many countries it is no longer the main goal, and certainly not the only goal.

Today, tribal people continue to face many problems. Centuries of prejudice and destruction of their land and resources have taken their toll. Once the resources are depleted, people can no longer live as their ancestors did. If prejudice limits their educational and job opportunities, they find themselves caught between two worlds. They are unable to support their families in traditional ways but lack the skills to survive in the cash economy around them. Their spirits suffer along with their bodies.

Many endangered tribal communities are now battling severe unemployment and the woes it breeds—violence and abuse of alcohol and other drugs.

But the picture is not completely bleak. Many governments are providing endangered groups with financial support, as well as assistance in housing, education, and medical services. Equally encouraging, hundreds of nongovernmental groups have been formed over the last decades to help tribal peoples save their lands and their cultures. Just as crucial, there is now a growing movement to respect and revive many ancient cultures, as people born into mainstream societies become aware of the fact that our natural resources include people.

And most important, tribal peoples are themselves becoming more vocal about their needs for self-determination, land rights, and cultural survival.

In the last chapter, we will explore some of the advances being made today on local, national, and international levels. But first you are invited to learn about five cultures that are presently endangered. These are the Yanomami (their name is also spelled *Yanomamo* and *Yanomama*) of the Amazon jungle in Brazil and Venezuela; the San (Bushmen) of the Kalahari Desert in southern Africa; the Bambuti (African Pygmies) of the Ituri Forest in Zaire, central Africa; the Aborigines of Australia; and the Inuits (Eskimos) of the Arctic and Subarctic regions.

Each of these groups, with its unique culture, religion, and history, represents a one-of-a-kind flowering of the human spirit. Each is a sample of our species' ingenuity, experience, and abilities. Each helps us realize how different human beings can be and at the same time gives us a mirror into which we can look and ask, Who is the real primitive here? While we struggle to master the advances in our technological society, each of these groups has exhibited great skill in reaping the natural resources of their own homelands. And the interpersonal skills of these groups struggling for survival often give citizens of today's fragmented "modern society" pause to think.

While outside forces threaten these tribal groups, more and more people are becoming aware of the importance of preserving these and other endangered cultures. First, there is the simple fact that we are all human and deserve the right to live in peace and retain our heritage. Each of us has a heritage that has helped to shape our own life and make us a part of the rich tapestry of our own society. More than likely, we are proud of this heritage and would not want to surrender it and the connectedness it gives us to others and to our past. By realizing our personal need for a heritage, perhaps we can understand the need that tribal people have for theirs, too.

On a more practical note, native people are privy to many secrets about the resources of their land, including the medicines and other products we can reap from them. More and more scientists are turning to them for their help. We can also learn about humankind's distant past by studying people who continue to live in the ways of our ancestors. Any tribal group that becomes extinct, culturally and/or physically, takes with it another link to that past and to our present, another reminder of how wide the human spectrum is.

In some cases, as with the Selk'nam (Onas) of

Tierra del Fuego, we cannot undo the wrongs that were done. Tierra del Fuego is a 17,000-square-mile (44,030 sq km) group of islands at the southern tip of South America. When Isla Grande, its largest island, was first settled by Europeans in 1870, the Ona on it numbered about 3,500. The European settlement proved to be their downfall. Newly imported diseases caused many natives to die, as did the violence between the Selk'nam and the immigrants who wanted their land. By 1929, there were fewer than 100 Selk'nam surviving. In 1973, a little more than 100 years after the first European settlement on Tierra del Fuego, the last Selk'nam passed away.[1]

As the number of tribes continues to dwindle, what we do now and how we think about other cultures become of critical importance. They will determine whether the tribal life-style will endure or whether the individual groups fighting for their lives today will go the way of the carrier pigeon, the Atlantic gray whale—and the Selk'nam.

YANOMAMI — of the — AMAZON RAIN FOREST

Perhaps the best known endangered tribe of recent years is the Yanomami Indians, the largest primitive group in existence today. The Yanomami live in southern Venezuela and northern Brazil, deep within the Amazon rain forest, which is the world's largest rain forest. As many people are well aware, the current destruction of the Amazon rain forest threatens many thousands of species of plants and animals. However, people generally do not realize that the rain forest's demise also threatens the Yanomami, and all the other tribes in the jungle who become victims of increased flooding, drought, and displacement, as well as disease and malnutrition brought about by deforestation.

Anthropologist Napoleon Chagnon, who spent over twenty-six years visiting and living among the Yanomami, calls them "our contemporary ancestors." This is because in many ways these people, whose name means in their own language "true human beings," are still living much like Stone Age

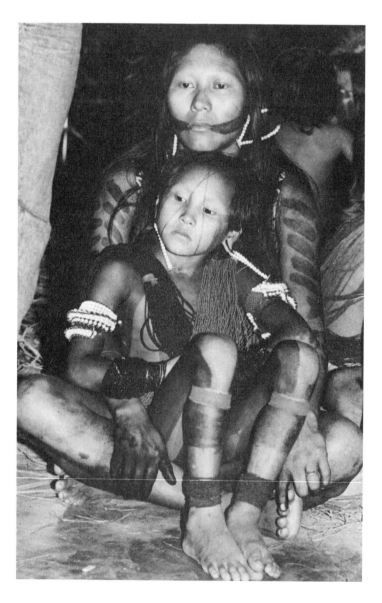

A Yanomami woman and her child, members of the world's largest remaining group of unacculturated tribal people, attend a meeting deep in the heart of the Amazon.

people did some 10,000 years ago, before farming changed civilization and ushered in the Iron Age.

Physically, these masters of the rain forest are short and slender, with straight black hair and high cheekbones. Their traditional everyday attire is either scanty or nonexistent. The Amazon's hot and humid climate makes most apparel more burdensome than essential. Since contact with Europeans, they may wear linen loincloths.

An estimated 5 million native Indians are believed to have been living in Brazil when the Portuguese landed there in 1500. However, the Yanomami weren't encountered by outsiders until 1800, when a famous German explorer and naturalist, Baron von Humbolt, reached their territory. For many years after their "discovery," the Yanomami were left alone because their inland homeland was deemed of no economic value. They were also not easily accessible. (In fact, early explorers called the Amazon rain forest a "green hell!") Their remoteness allowed the Yanomami to continue living as they had for centuries.

The Yanomami are gardeners as well as hunter-gatherers who hunt wild animals and gather wild plants. The mainstay of their diet is provided by their gardens, in which their primary crops are plantains and bananas, supplemented by sugarcane, avocados, and sweet potatoes. They also cultivate hallucinogens (mind-altering drugs), which the men use to contact mountain spirits who help them cure illnesses. They raise cotton and tobacco. The cotton is used to make articles of clothing and decoration, as well as the hammocks the Yanomami sleep in. Tobacco is chewed frequently during the day by everyone, including children.

Hunting animals and gathering wild plants add variety to the Yanomami life-style, and the men never leave their village without their bows and a variety of arrows. Bows were traditionally made with wood from palm trees, and arrows were made from bamboo and other plants, but since contact with outsiders and with tribes who traded with outsiders, metal weapons have also come into use.

With these weapons, the Yanomami hunt many animals, including monkeys, their most common source of meat. Some of the other animals sought are armadillos and tapirs, heavy-bodied vegetarians that resemble pigs. Among the birds hunted are curassows, whose quills are used to feather arrows. The Yanomami's weapons also protect them from poisonous snakes and jaguars, as well as from enemy raiding parties.

Yanomami live in small communities with an average population of seventy-five people, all dwelling in a continuous circular house known as a *shabano*. Built around a central courtyard, the *shabano* has a roof of leaves and is by no means a permanent structure. Every few years, the *shabano* decays, a victim of insects, personal garbage, and general wear and tear. When that happens, it must be taken down and rebuilt.

Within the *shabano*, each family has its own section, and groups of families are arranged according to kinship and lineage. Families have a separate woven hammock for each family member. These are hung around the family hearth, over which cooking is done. A fire burns in the hearth throughout the night to keep everyone warm. As the weather gets colder, sleepers may get up occasionally to tend the

A Yanomami hunter has successfully speared his prey. He rarely ventures from his village without an arsenal of weapons.

blaze, and some brave souls may go to the natural bathroom around the shabano, but nobody ventures very far after dark, because the jungle is a dangerous place.

Since there are no partitions between the hearths, there is little privacy in the shabano. As in some thin-walled apartment buildings in North American cities, everyone here knows everyone else's business. Each family's quarrels, as well as its jokes, are heard and seen by all. In this world of few secrets, the result of a heated argument between a husband and wife might be that everyone gives the couple advice.

A family's residence in the open-roofed, unpartitioned circular house known as a shabano

It is not considered unusual for an inhabitant of the *shabano* to be up until dawn making a speech to the whole community about something he or she is concerned about. Others are not forced to listen, and unless the talk is keeping everyone up, the speaker may go on all night, without considering others discourteous if they turn away in their hammocks and go to sleep.

Although these Yanomami villages are independent, self-reliant entities, social obligations are the cornerstone of Yanomami society. Villages often host feasts for other villages; they may serve such typical feast fare as boiled plantain soup, smoked monkeys, and wild turkey. It is not unusual for guests to travel many days on foot through winding jungle trails to reach the host village. These visits take place mainly during the dry season, from September through April, because the heavy tropical downpours of the rainy season isolate many groups.

Feasts are times for cementing social, political, and economic links between communities. The hosts generally give the visitors a gift, such as a pot, a machete, hallucinogens, or food. In return, the visiting village is expected to reciprocate with a feast for their hosts, as well as a gift for them. Should the reciprocal agreement be unfulfilled, the result could be the start of a war that might be passed on, much as their myths are, from generation to generation.

Warfare among the Yanomami is common, as Napoleon Chagnon informed the world with his books and articles about these people. Although missionaries had been in the area since 1950, the world at large knew very little about the Yanomami until after 1964, when Chagnon first went to South

America to study them. At that time he was a graduate student of anthropology at the University of Michigan. (He is currently a professor at the University of California at Santa Barbara.)

Chagnon's months of research led to the publication of a book that has become a college classic and has shaped the way outsiders view the Yanomami. In his book, *Yanomamo: The Fierce People*, Chagnon explains that this is a title the Yanomami hold with great pride: being known as "warlike" is an honor for them. One of their myths may help to explain this attitude.

According to the myth, long ago the people were angry at Moon, who ate the souls of children. An ancestor called Suhirina shot Moon with a bamboo-tipped arrow. It pierced Moon, causing blood to spill all over the earth. From this blood, say the Yanomami, human beings were created. Because they come from Moon's blood, men are fierce and must fight. The stronger were created from Moon's blood that spilled from the center; the weaker came from Moon's droplets.

Warfare for the Yanomami can range in fierceness from chest-pounding duels between groups to battles with clubs or spears to raids and ambushes. The duels, in which each man pounds on the other man's chest, follow very strict rules about exactly how to give and receive these blows. Battles with clubs or spears are more dangerous; raids are more deadly. Each man who participates in a raid intends to kill at least one enemy and escape without being captured. Most cruel of all are ambushes, in which an unsuspecting village is tricked into relaxing at a feast set up by a second village. While they are enjoying themselves, they are attacked by a third village, who has planned the ambush with the host village.

When a village spreads bad rumors about another village, that is a minor offense punishable by a chest-pounding duel. Greater consequences will result from being caught having an affair or stealing food. Either crime could lead to a raid that would have serious implications for generations to come, since revenge would inevitably follow.

However, warfare is only one aspect of the Yanomami life-style. Dr. Kenneth Good, the author of *Into the Heart*, a recent book about the Yanomami, advises people to avoid portraying the Yanomami as brutish, a label he feels is unfair and does not keep their life-style in perspective. Dr. Good, currently a professor of anthropology at Jersey City State University in New Jersey, first traveled to Venezuela as a graduate student to study a group of Yanomami for fifteen months. His stay extended for twelve years, during which time he got to know them in depth and married a Yanomami woman with whom he now has two children.

Dr. Good is not blind to the brutalities he saw around him, but he also witnessed many displays of tenderness among the Yanomami. Like Dr. Chagnon, Good told of a society in which people joke, chatter, and gossip much like people back in the States. In fact, Good reached the conclusion that labeling the Yanomami the "fierce people" is like calling New Yorkers "the mugging and murdering people."

From Chagnon and other anthropologists, the world has learned about a village society in which the top official is the headman, generally the most able and gifted of the tribe. For the Yanomami, though, prestige and persuasion work better than outright authority.

The next most important person in the Yanomami community is the *shaman*, or medicine man, who is called upon to cure diseases. He does this primarily by communicating with the ageless spirits, known as the *hekuri*, who the Yanomami believe are living in the mountains. Contacting the *hekuri* is most often done by chanting after taking special drugs that induce visions. These mind-altering drugs come from a variety of rain forest plants, including hisiome seeds and the bark of the epene tree. After the seeds or bark has been ground into a fine powder, the drug is blown into a person's nose through a long hollow tube. Taking drugs is associated with curing illnesses, and abusing drugs is frowned upon.

The shaman also cures diseases by forcibly re-moving them from the victim's body with massages or by sucking on the injured or ill place, a method used by many tribal groups, including American Indians. Because the *hekuri* reportedly love beauty, the shamans decorate themselves with beautiful paints and exotic bird feathers. Other tribal mem-bers adorn their own bodies for feasts, for the few festivals the Yanomami hold, and often at the end of the workday as well. For women, a special sign of beauty is the slender, polished sticks piercing the nose, corners of the mouth, and middle of the lip.

The roles of the sexes for the Yanomami are clearly defined. There is no Yanomami women's lib-eration movement. The men are the leaders of the

Above: *The seeds or bark of a hallucinatory drug are ground into a fine powder. The men then blow the powder up each other's nostrils through a hollow tube, and chant to the forest spirits as the drug takes effect.*
Below: *Two Yanomami teenage girls wear one of the tribe's signs of beauty, thin polished sticks that pierce the face.*

community and the shamans. They are also expected to tend the garden and do the hunting, for which they coat their arrows with a poison such as *curare*. Curare comes from a wild jungle vine and is primarily used to paralyze the big spider monkeys so that they fall from the trees.

The women are also important to the economic life of the village. They are expected to gather the wild plants, such as palm fruits, brazil nuts, and wild bananas; collect the various insects they eat; and cook and serve the food. They are responsible for gathering firewood for the family hearth, a job that takes several hours of labor daily. They must search out the wood, then haul heavy loads of it back home. Although the men may accompany the women to make sure that other tribes do not kidnap them (many tribes have a woman shortage), the women are still expected to do all the carrying.

When an area's resources are exhausted, everyone in the village may leave on a trek known as a *wayumi*. The men will go first to hunt, while the women follow close behind, with huge baskets on their backs containing basic necessities. These include their hammocks; gourds, which are used as containers for drinking water; and leaves to make a roof for temporary housing.

Childhood for both sexes seems to be a happy, carefree time spent playing in the jungle, often in games that imitate adult activities. Games include catching bees and using a bow and tiny arrows to shoot at such targets as crickets, small rodents, and lizards on a string. The children may also pretend to blow hallucinogenic drugs into each others' noses, using ashes instead. Other games include playing catch with an inflated anteater bladder and chasing fireflies at night. Reportedly, children are seldom punished, and parents tend to be indulgent though they are diligent in teaching children basic Yanomami values: to share with their friends but to take vengeance for aggression. It is not unusual for parents to urge their youngsters to avenge themselves when hurt by another child, even if the incident is an accident. Sexuality is not repressed, and sexual relations before marriage are considered natural.

When it is time to consider marriage, available partners are those for whom no incest taboos exist. In Yanomami society, marriage can only take place between a man and a woman of two different lineages. There are only two lineages in each village, and each child belongs to his or her father's lineage.

As a Yanomami girl grows up, her family may betrothe (engage) her to several different men. Each man is usually much older than she is and an active hunter in the village. When a girl is betrothed, she becomes the man's special friend. This often happens at a young age; Dr. Good's wife was only eight when her mother betrothed her to him. After betrothal, a girl's responsibilities are tending the man's fire and occasionally bringing him food. Sexual favors are not necessarily part of the arrangement.

No matter how much a Yanomami girl may care for a man, she cannot marry until she begins to menstruate. At the onset of her menses she goes through the most important ceremony of her life. Now she must retreat to an isolated house made of leaves from the yupi tree. During her seclusion there, she observes traditional food taboos. Then other women in her family help her dress in a traditional outfit, and when she walks across the village plaza in her dress and cotton armbands she is announcing to the whole community that she has come of age and is ready to marry.

Her choice of a mate is revealed when she hangs her hammock next to that of the man she has selected. Her chosen husband may be one of the men she has been betrothed to or someone to whom she has never been engaged. Because of the shortage of women among the Yanomami, it is seldom that a man refuses to marry the woman who has selected him.

When a Yanomami woman is ready to give birth, she goes into the forest, away from the immediate neighborhood, with a midwife to help. Later, the new mother's husband comes to take her and their new baby home. As parents, the Yanomami are reportedly devoted to their children, although child care is primarily a woman's concern. Mothers nurse their offspring and sleep in the same hammock with them until the children are about four years old.

However, anthropologists who have lived among the tribe report that relationships between husbands and wives are anything but idyllic. Husbands will beat their wives if they disobey, and it is not unusual for wives to have several scars. Sarcasm in public is another form of marital abuse. There is a double standard in Yanomami society—it is acceptable for a man to have many other women, but a wife caught with another man can expect a severe beating from her husband.

When a Yanomami dies, the people have a custom that is unusual to those of us in the Western world. After a loved one's body is cremated, the ashes are mixed with ripe plantains into a soup or-drink consumed at a funeral feast by relatives and others wishing to show respect. After a person dies, his or her name is no longer spoken, a custom known to have been practiced until very recently by several North American Indian groups. Even when a person is alive, Yanomamis prefer that the name he or she was given at birth not be spoken: doing so can send the person addressed into a rage.

CHANGES

Even by the time Chagnon first visited the Yanomami, the winds of change and destruction had begun to blow. Missionaries had already introduced the people to machetes, metal cooking utensils, shotguns—and epidemics of measles and malaria. Subtle attacks on their culture were under way, as missionaries encouraged the people to convert to Christianity.

After Chagnon's initial contact, gold miners and tin prospectors began arriving in growing numbers, since the area is rich in mineral wealth. As their numbers swelled, national and international groups pressured the Brazilian government to set up a re-serve for the Yanomami. Their request appeared to be granted in 1982, when the Brazilian government established a Yanomami reserve that consisted of over 19 million acres (7.7 million hectares) of land. Supposedly, the tribe was free to practice its tradi-tional life-style here.

The government was not being altruistic: officials actually were more interested in prospering from gaining control over all the Yanomami's land and its minerals. The Yanomami had more "sky rights" than land rights, being promised "exclusive possession of the open sky." From their viewpoint, they had their hunting and gathering grounds and everything seemed fine.

The Yanomami were not to be left alone for long. In 1987, a Brazilian government study reported that gold, tin, diamonds, and bauxite had been found in Yanomami territory, Roraimo State, Brazil. This news quickly drew swarms of prospectors into an area then inhabited by approximately 9,000 Yanomami. According to newspaper reports, some 40,000 prospectors, known as *garimpeiros*, have poured into the Yanomami's mineral-rich land in the last few years.

The newcomers brought with them imported diseases that have killed as many as 1,500 Yanomami, since the people lack immunity to the outsiders' illnesses. Even the common cold can prove deadly to them. Many have become seriously ill or have died from outbreaks of measles, tuberculosis, sexually transmitted diseases, and malaria. In Brazil, many Yanomami have also fallen sick from the handouts of food they get from miners, because the food is alien to their diet.

Physical fights with miners have also caused many deaths, both of miners and of Yanomami. In addition, miners have polluted the area with the mercury used to separate the gold when they panned the rivers for it. Fish in the rivers are contaminated, as are plants along the water's edge that absorb the mercury around them. These plants are eaten by people as well as by jungle animals that people later eat, causing mercury poisoning either directly or indirectly.

The prospectors are a mixed group. Some represent huge corporate interests, while others are simple people hoping to strike it rich to provide better for their families. But regardless of what motivates these intruders, the Yanomami have suffered from their presence. The natural resources and game animals upon which their livelihood is based are dwindling, and the Brazilian Yanomami face serious survival problems.

In 1989, the Brazilian government then in power issued a series of decrees that reduced the Yanomami lands from 23 million to 5 million acres (4.3 to 2 million hectares). As a result, the people were left with nineteen scattered areas, less than 30 percent of the original Yanomami land. The rest of their land was turned into state-run national parks and forests. The next year, however, the tide turned.

In 1990, the newly elected Brazilian government under the leadership of President Fernando Collor de Mello, promised to evict the estimated 45,000 prospectors on Yanomami land. The plan was put into action with the dynamiting of 120 hidden jungle airplane landing strips used to carry supplies to mining sites. (Many jungle trees had been cut down to build these strips.) This bombing campaign was part of President Collor de Mello's "Operation Free Yanomami Jungle."[1] The Brazilian president also revoked the 1989 decrees, although he had not yet given the Yanomami formal possession of the land when he was impeached for corruption in October 1992.

Many anthropologists are pessimistic about the future of the Yanomami in Brazil, but matters are more hopeful in Venezuela. There, the government of President Carlos Andres Perez has recently shown a desire to prevent a repetition of the Brazilian tragedy. President Perez has expelled hundreds of miners, created an army post to patrol the border area, and given the Yanomami rights to their land.

In 1990, Dr. Chagnon and others surveyed the Yanomami on a trip sponsored by the Venezuelan government as a preliminary to creating the Siapa River Valley Biosphere, a tribal reserve where "the Yanomami can live according to their traditional ways without interference from gold miners or missionaries." During this trip, Chagnon and his fellow travelers reported finding ten Yanomami villages that had not been contacted by outsiders.[2]

A year later, during the summer of 1991, President Perez signed a decree that reserved a 32,038-square-mile (82,980 sq-km) stretch of Amazon forest (about the size of Maine) as a permanent homeland for Venezuela's 14,000 Yanomami. According to President Perez, "The primary use will be to preserve and to learn the traditional ways of the Indians." Anthropologists and other defenders of the Yanomami were delighted with the decree.[3] As Dr. Chagnon recently said, "Hopefully, the President of Brazil will take the example of President Perez and do something similar to demarcate land in Brazil for the Yanomami on that side of the border."

In Brazil, Indian-rights activists continue their twenty-year struggle to set up a reserve for the Yanomami surviving there. But the road ahead continues to be bumpy, and if the Yanomami are to

— 30 —

Above: Yanomami children listen with rapt attention to a tape deck brought by health workers to a remote region of the Brazilian Amazon. It plays music recorded at other Yanomami communities, and speeches by Indian leaders opposing the presence of gold prospectors. Below: A Yanomami woman is fascinated by a lipstick brought by gold and diamond prospectors, who have also brought such deadly diseases as measles and malaria, to which the Yanomami have no resistance.

survive as a people, they must be helped on many fronts. They need to be vaccinated against imported diseases, which is a difficult task since their settlements are spread out over thousands of square miles. They need guaranteed land rights wherever they live, with total control, to maintain their trade networks and hunting grounds. They also need their diet monitored so that they do not become ill from food supplied by miners and other outsiders.

Is it worth it? ask some people. Why not simply assimilate the Yanomami into mainstream Brazilian and Venezuelan society? Wouldn't this be best for them? Some cultural anthropologists answer yes; others hope that if assimilation does happen, it is not before they can study the impact on the Yanomami of an agricultural revolution stimulated by the introduction of steel tools. This would set up a kind of artificial Iron Age that could help us grasp our own ancestors' major life-style changes. Then again, how can we really know what is best for the Yanomami until we see the world from their perspective?

Perhaps the Yanomami's perspective is best revealed in a report that comes not from the Amazon, but from New York City. In April 1991, *The New York Times*[4] reported on the travels of Davi Kopenawa Yanomami, the first Brazilian Yanomami to visit the United States. Brought here by an Indian-rights group, he had the mission of speaking for his people. Davi is one of the few Yanomami who can speak Portuguese, the primary language of Brazil. Among the groups he addressed was the Secretary General of the United Nations in New York City.

Davi found being in Manhattan a bewildering experience. "They look all the time at the ground and never see the sky. Why do they do that?" Davi asked, baffled by the sight of people scurrying past him on the city streets. To him, New Yorkers were quite strange indeed.

While we pause to reflect on how we must appear to the Yanomami, new organizations are working to help these people survive. Dr. Chagnon reports that he is deeply involved in initiating two new programs in Venezuela to assist the Yanomami as well as neighboring tribes who are beginning to suffer from the effects of the Brazilian gold rush. Venezuelans, who have a higher standard of living than Brazilians, have shown little interest in gold mining in the Amazon. But Brazilians who were expelled from their country's Yanomami lands are spilling over into Venezuelan territory. Chagnon has created a fund-raising organization, the Yanomami Survival Fund. He is also affiliated with several other groups, including the recently formed American Friends of Venezuelan Indians (AFVI). According to Dr. Chagnon, these two groups "are going to have the most enduring and effective programs for the Yanomami."

This famous anthropologist's own experience with the Yanomami and other Indian tribes has led him to believe that "the future of any child anywhere is guaranteed only if the lands they live on are pro- tected for the future of their culture."

SAN (BUSHMEN) of the KALAHARI DESERT

In the 1984 movie *The Gods Must Be Crazy*, the San (Bushmen) of the magnificent Kalahari Desert of Africa are romanticized as innocent hunter-gatherers who are forced to confront the craziness of the civilized world. Their adventures begin when a Coke bottle thrown from an airplane lands in their campsite and starts a string of sometimes hilarious, other times violent, events.

Jaime Uys, the film's South African writer, producer, and director, traveled around the world with his star performer, N!Xau, a charming San who made his appearances wearing animal skins. Uys told the press that he had found N!Xau out in the bush hunting and gathering with his people and had persuaded him to be in the film.

However, American anthropologist and documentary filmmaker John Marshall has been very annoyed by the publicity surrounding the movie and its 1989 sequel. According to Mr. Marshall, who has been studying, filming, and helping the San for over forty years, N!Xau never hunted and gathered in his life. The same can be said for almost all of the San living today. With that in mind, let us focus on the *real* San and discover why they are endangered.

To set the record straight, "Bushmen" is a term the San consider derogatory; it was given to them by Dutch settlers some 300 years ago. *San*, which means "original people," is preferred, although the San would rather be called by their particular division, which include the !Kung, Kua/Gwi, and !XO. Other San groups are the Kukwe, Korana, Korkoko, Nama, and Namib. The San in *The Gods Must Be Crazy* are the !Kung, the exclamation point symbolizing the click sound in their language. All of the San groups are distinguished by languages with clicks and pops, and since we are discussing many such groups in this chapter, San is the most appropriate term to use.

The San are considered an extremely talkative people; conversing is said to be their favorite pastime. They like to tell stories, savoring every detail. In their hunter-gatherer days, when the nights were cold they would stay up chatting until the next morning, not even attempting to sleep until the sun came out and warmed them. Only one subject was taboo, the spirits of the dead, which the San still believe are responsible for bringing illnesses and misfortune to the tribe.

In physical appearance, the San are short in stature; the men little taller than five feet and the women even shorter. Considered graceful, they have thin, wiry bodies with long, slender arms and legs. Their skin is a light yellow-brown that darkens and

Known as a talkative people, a group of San share lengthy stories and gossip with each other.

wrinkles with age as a result of their daily encounters with the blazing sunlight and constant dust.

Their clothing before contact with Europeans consisted primarily of animal skins. Men wore a leather loincloth, women a small leather apron and a leather cape known as a *kaross*. Made from animal hide, the *kaross* can be tied to form a pouch in back for carrying a baby or ostrich eggs. The eggs were emptied by blowing out the insides, and then used as water carriers. Today, San also wear European clothes made of cloth, which are warmer and more comfortable than leather. The ostrich-eggshell beads they once used to string in tiny bands and wear around their arms and knees for ornamentation have largely been replaced by colored glass beads. But the women still beautify themselves with etchings on their foreheads and thighs.

The San are considered among the earliest human inhabitants who still live in southern Africa. Perhaps as long as 20,000 years ago their ancestors roamed freely in a land that must have been a hunter-gatherer's paradise, rich with enough animals and plants to satisfy any Stone Age appetite. They lived across much of south and eastern Africa, their range extending across hills and valleys, riverbanks, deserts, and grasslands. And until the Hottentots emerged in southern Africa about 2,000 to 4,000 years ago, the San appear to have had the land much to themselves. The Hottentot shared many linguistic and physical similarities with the light-skinned San but with an important major difference: Besides hunting and gathering, the Hottentots herded cattle, goats, and sheep. Since herds need grazing land, wild game in their vicinity were forced to abandon the area, leaving the San without their main source of protein.

The San either moved to more plentiful hunting areas or killed the newcomers' animals. They did not consider killing someone else's animals to be a crime, because they thought of all animals as fair game. The concept of owning an animal was foreign to them. Then, too, they considered any animals

— 37 —

grazing on their land as their own because each San group had a particular territory for hunting purposes, which all other San groups respected.

The clashes between San and Hottentot were echoed in the third century, when the Bantu reached their land from the north. The Bantu are black Africans who speak the Bantu languages. Although the Bantu and the San initially coexisted peacefully, the peace did not last. As more and more Bantu arrived and began confiscating San lands for herding and farming, friction grew. Unfortunately for the San, the newcomers were much more powerful.

Then came the Europeans. The first Europeans to arrive in the region were Portuguese sailors in the fifteenth century. By the seventeenth century, the Dutch and the British were the main newcomers, landing along the coast on trading voyages. They traded with the Hottentots, exchanging iron, copper, tobacco, alcohol, and beads for the tribe's ivory, ostrich feathers, and cattle. By 1652, the Dutch had made their first permanent settlement at the Cape. Soon, the 300,000 San then in South Africa would begin rapidly declining in numbers.

The Hottentots complained to the Dutch about the "savage" San. Because the Dutch wanted to keep the Hottentots as friendly exchange partners, they

Two young San men wear the traditional dress as well as modern European clothing. These pictures tell the story of a people caught at a crossroads in their history.

accepted their opinion as valid. Further confirmation came when the Dutch began raising sheep and cattle on San territory and the San killed these animals.

In response to San raids on European farms, European soldiers were sent in and many San were killed. Throughout the eighteenth century, the conflict between colonists and San intensified. Since the colonists had the guns, the San suffered the most casualties. Thousands were killed or taken prisoner and made slaves. As the century drew to a close, the British annexed the Cape (1795) and any San not killed or made a serf were pushed farther and farther north.

By the beginning of the twentieth century, almost all of the surviving San were confined to one place: a 600,000-square-mile stretch of African desert known as the Kalahari. Located primarily in Botswana and Namibia, this inhospitable land also reaches into South Africa and central Angola. It is often barren except for the great baobab trees (sometimes called elephant trees because of their shape) that can live for 2,000 years or more. These trees serve as landmarks in a region of constant droughts with an average rainfall that varies from 4 to 16 inches (100 to 400 milliliters). It is a land where the annual drought generally ends in December with the start of the three-month rainy season; June and July are winter months.

The only hills here are the *Tsodillo*, a name that means slippery. Located in northwest Botswana, these natural structures are considered sacred by the San. The !Kung San who live in northern Botswana and adjacent areas of Namibia and Angola say that the hills were made by their great god, who painted the ancient pictures of animals on the rocks. Zebras, giraffes, rhinoceros, and many different antelopes are pictured; the animal most often painted is the eland bull, the biggest of Africa's antelopes. The San believe that the eland has the greatest supernatural power of any creature.

In all, thousands of pictures remain at Tsodillo. Like the other exquisitely executed paintings found in mountain caves and on sheltered rocks through-out southern Africa and attributed to the San, these artworks continue to amaze scholars, who wonder how the artists created long-lasting paints that could withstand heat, glaring light, and wind for centuries. Scholars are equally baffled by the ancient artists' ability to handle perspective and capture animated motion as well as they did. The paintings and en-gravings that remain serve as a legacy, revealing scenes from the San's life and capturing their re-markable artistic and poetic skills.

The San are also deemed remarkable for their outstanding strategies for surviving in the Kalahari. As late as the 1950s, many San were still able to live as hunter-gatherers, extracting the very last drop of water from a land of miserly rainfall. Today, their desert skills are mostly memories: Although an esti-mated 50,000 to 60,000 San still exist, no more than about 1,000 maintain a semblance of their tradi-tional life-style as hunters and gatherers. Those who are closest to this customary existence live in the 20,000-square-mile (51,775-sq-km) Central Kala-hari Reserve in Botswana, set aside for the San in 1961. In the rest of the Botswana Kalahari, and in Namibia, most San have been pressured into settling down in one place, at or within easy reach of a waterhole. Dispossessed of their land and unable

—41—

and often unwilling to live as their ancestors did, the San are in severe danger of becoming culturally extinct. Yet movies and articles continue to spread myths about their supporting themselves by hunting and gathering as they did in the past.

In reality, the people try to hold on to the spirit of sharing which they had in their nomadic days, but it is not easy to do. In traditional San culture, cooperation was essential. People were expected to share the plants they gathered and the small animals they hunted with their immediate family, and to share bigger game animals with the whole band. The few possessions each family had were also shared, usually among tribal members with barter ties to each other.

Before resettlement on reservations, the San's basic social unit was a small band consisting of no more than fifty people, small enough not to exhaust the resources around them. Each band had its own territory in which it could use any of the natural resources available, but band membership was fluid. Bands frequently broke up and recombined with other small bands, generally either to help their hunt or to resolve an argument between two people in the same band.

The bands moved from waterhole to waterhole, gradually fanning out farther and farther from their home base to hunt animals and gather plants until they depleted the food supply in their area. Then they moved on to find another waterhole at which to set up camp before they migrated into more arid sections of the desert once again.

Their camps, known as *werfs*, consisted of individual dome-shaped huts. These shelters, called *scherms*, are still used today, although European-

— **42** —

style houses are also seen in the Kalahari. *Scherms* are traditionally made of grass and poles and are built in a circle around a central communal area. The whole community used to pitch in to build a family's hut. However, the huts were rarely slept in. Family possessions were kept in the huts, but family members huddled at night around the fire in the hearth outside. Today, traditional huts and the mud-

Although traditional San build a shelter known as a scherm, they sleep outside the structure. *Today, San are just as likely to be found living in European-style housing.*

walled structures that have replaced them are more likely to be built facing away from each other, and family fires are made inside. Both changes are signs of the new attitude of the tribe.

In the past, bands had either no leaders or a headman whose obvious wisdom and abilities made him a natural leader. But the band's medicine men usually commanded greater respect than any headman. It is estimated that today, as in the past, as many as half the males in a band are medicine men at some point in their lives, keeping their title until they lose the power to heal. In the past, medicine men had various specialties, such as leading hunters to plentiful game, bringing rain, or foretelling the future. Today, San medicine men are primarily involved in curing illnesses.

The San remains a very egalitarian society. In the past, the women were crucial to their band's economic life, because the men's hunting expeditions were usually less successful than the women's gathering forays. Roots, bulbs, tubers, and fruit made up 60 to 80 percent of the food by weight, and the women were able to recognize more than 100 edible plants. This knowledge was a necessity for survival because the availability of foods in the Kalahari could vary dramatically from season to season.

About half of the vegetable diet in the northern Kalahari consisted of the mongongo nut, an abundant, and protein-rich, marvel of nature that resists drought and can be harvested for as much as a year after it has fallen from the tree. Two other important plants in the past were tsama melons and wild turnips. Tsama melons were the main source of food and most water for San during droughts. The meat from these smooth, shiny green plants was boiled, and the seeds were roasted and eaten or were ground into powder and used as flour. The rinds served several purposes: as containers, cooking pots, and mixing bowls. Children used them as drums and as targets for their shooting practice.

The fibrous wild turnips, known as "bi," were also a major source of water in the dry season, especially to San who weren't living near a waterhole. Bi grows all year, although its bitter taste makes it less desirable than the tsama and other melons. In the past, the San were also proficient at obtaining water by squeezing it out of the stomachs of the animals they killed and by using the hollow stem of a desert plant to sip it from the hollows of trees.

Until the 1950s, although the men might occasionally help the women gather plants, their main occupation was hunting. The principal animals they sought were large antelopes such as the eland, gemsbok, hartebeest, and wildebeeste, as well as the wart hog, porcupine, steenbok, springhare, and duiker, a little nocturnal antelope no larger than a small dog. Although most young San no longer hunt, during the last few years there has been a gradual revival of the time-honored hunting skills of the elders. Such skills include the ability to recognize the trail of a wounded animal at a glance. Those who are most observant can find a cold trail even over stones. The hunters also know not to say the animal's name out loud, for to do so would give the wounded creature strength to recover.

Other hunting skills to master in the Kalahari include attracting a mother animal by imitating the cry of its young and approaching a flock of ostriches by shaping a stick to resemble an ostrich's neck. Traditionally, hunters would stalk an animal for

—45—

Left: *San women and children gather plants. As vegetation in their area diminishes, the women's extensive knowledge of plant life is lost and their equality with their husbands suffers.* Below: *Hunting game with bow and arrows, once part of the traditional way of life for the San, has become increasingly rare.*

hours before it could be shot with a poisoned arrow. After the arrow blade went through the animal's skin, the creature might travel on for as long as a day or more until the poison took effect. During that time, the hunter had to try to lure the victim toward his camp so that when it finally fell, he did not have to carry it too far. Skillful hunters took great precautions so that the animal did not panic too soon, which could speed up the poison's work, downing the animal while still a long walk from the camp.

In the past, like the women, the men spent less than half the week pursuing food. This gave them much free time to enjoy leisure activities such as chatting around the fire, playing games, visiting other camps, and entertaining visitors to their own campsite. Today, life is much different. Where hunting is practiced, it is often done with four-wheel-drive vehicles and high-powered rifles rather than with bows and arrows, which are now made primarily to sell to tourists.

Just as men do not dominate women in San society, parents do not dominate children. San children are seldom disciplined, and their education continues to be primarily what they hear by listening to the arguments and discussions of the adults around them. In this way, children learn about their family's history, and how to handle their kinship and barter ties. But the games they play no longer prepare them for the adult roles they will assume someday. While boys may continue to play games of chase and shoot bows and arrows and spears, they are generally not being prepared for a life of hunting.

In traditional households, marriage continues to take place for San girls after their fifteenth birthday, or sometimes much sooner. Even before a girl is able to walk, her parents might promise the parents of a boy perhaps five years her senior that she will marry him when she comes of age. This practice is based on the San belief that stable marriages are more possible when a man is allowed to raise his wife to be. The young men are expected to abstain from sex with their future wife until she is ready to be married.

Men traditionally marry in their early twenties. In the past, a marriage would not take place until the young man had proved to the bride's family that he was able to hunt, and thus support a wife, as well as her parents in their old age. The young man demonstrated his ability by giving the girl's parents his first large animal, which he had to kill in order to go through the Rite of the First Kill ritual. In the past, the rite and the presentation of meat to his future in-laws were pivotal male "coming of age" initiations; no male was considered a man unless he married, and no marriage was allowed unless the Rite of the First Kill had taken place.

However, long before these initiations, boys of eight or so used to go through a voluntary male initiation ceremony called *choma*. It was held every four or five years during the winter, and only boys who had shot their first buck could be initiated. They were recognized afterward by the unique haircut they received as part of the ceremony. Today, fewer and fewer boys voluntarily undergo *choma*, and the Rite of the First Kill is seldom performed.

Girls continue to participate in ceremonies when they come of age to bear children, which has a natural marker: the start of their menses. If a girl is engaged at a very young age, she will usually continue living with her parents until menstruation begins. As in many tribal groups, a San female's first menstrual cycle calls for a certain period of isolation as an initiation. During this time she will be taught how she should act as a wife and mother. After a girl's initiation, she wears red paint around her eyes as a sign that she is free to marry.

If a family keeps San traditions, when a couple is ready to marry, the mothers of the bride and groom build a *scherm* for the young couple and unite the couple with special rituals. For her wedding day, the bride wears a special costume and has her hair arranged in a bridal cap of flattened, uncurled fringes around her head. Around her neck she wears a necklace of ostrich-shell disks, as well as animal teeth and special herbs. The wedding, like other San ceremonies, is not held until after the sun has gone down, since the San associate the sun with death.

After their wedding, a San couple will live with the girl's family during the early part of their marriage. Later, if they wish, they will be free to live with the husband's family. Traditionally, a man is allowed to have as many wives as he can afford. However, a man usually can afford only one wife at a time, or two at the most.

In the past, when it was time for a San woman to give birth, she usually did so alone, at some distance from the campsite. She was expected to endure her pain bravely, although a woman having her first child might be helped by her mother or another woman. Afterward, the mother marked the spot where she gave birth so that men could avoid it. According to the San, any man who stepped on the spot might lose his ability to hunt.

Death, like birth, continues to call for special rituals. The !Kung bury their dead in a sitting position after binding the body. When the burial is finished, they break down the dead person's *scherm* over the grave, along with his possessions, then strew an aromatic powder known as *sasa* over it. It is traditionally believed that sprinkling the *sasa* keeps away the spirits of the dead, which travel in whirlwinds and are known as *gauas*. In the past, a band would move its whole camp after a person in it was buried. In the words of N!ai, a young San woman profiled in the documentary *N!ai, the Story of a !Kung Woman*, "We left sickness behind us when we moved." After the San were dispossessed of their land and forced to give up their nomadic ways, the practice of moving after a burial ceased; as a result, the San were faced with many sanitation problems.

For the living, dancing remains an important activity. San dances serve many purposes, from expressing hunger to giving thanks to an animal for allowing itself to be killed. One of the San's best known dances is the trance cure, in which power is summoned from the cosmos to heal the sick. This marathon dance lasts all night and, like other dances, is a social and recreational event as well as an opportunity for healings. Trance dancers heal by laying their hands on everyone present.

Held at night, trance dances generally have a central fire that is kept burning throughout the ceremony. A circle of performers consisting of women singers sits near the fire. Behind them, the dancers moving in a circle are predominantly male, although women may dance if they wish. The rattles tied on each dancer's ankles have been carefully made from dried cocoons strung together with sinew cords. As many as sixty cocoons are contained in each rattle that swishes as the dancers move. Since the rattles are expected to last a lifetime, they are very carefully tended between dances.

While the women clap their hands, they sing wordless medicine songs that honor the game animals. Like the dance steps, the songs are learned from childhood on. Although the dance begins with casual steps, the dancers are expected to continue dancing for hours, until they reach the point of exhaustion. Then, unable to dance any longer, some dancers enter into a trance state, often shrieking and collapsing.

Each dancer in a trance is placed on the ground outside the dance circle. While some dancers go on with their performance, others attend to the person in a trance, rubbing his body with their hands and with their heads until he literally shines with their sweat. For the San, sweat is a key ingredient of this dance: it represents medicine. In order to be effective, the San curer must sweat, even though his patient need not.

When a trance dancer is ready, he lays his hands on all the people at the dance, in order to suck the evil from their bodies. Illnesses and misfortune brought by the spirits of the dead and other hostile forces are believed to be transferred from the patient's body to that of the medicine men. Once the illness is transferred, it can be released, to return to the spirits of the dead once more. Sick people receive extra attention during trance dances, as many curers may work on a sick person, by turns or together.

According to Elizabeth Thomas, John Marshall's sister and the author of *The Harmless People*, a book about her experiences among the San, the spirits of the dead are themselves dancers who are visible whenever the moon has a ring around it. The ring is made by their feet as they dance and the moon is their dance fire.

CHANGES

As mentioned earlier, the poetry and history of the San are revealed in the rich samples of art that are thousands of years old and found in Botswana, Namibia, and South Africa, as well as in Zimbabwe, Zambia, and Angola. Besides the many animals the artists painted, there are more recent San drawings of the ships Europeans came in, and the seventeenth-century Dutch farmers' wagons and livestock. Raids on livestock were also painted, as were the British soldiers in uniform.

The first settlement in Natal was established by English traders in 1824. Thirteen years later, several thousand Dutch colonists, known as Boers, set up their own republic in Natal in an effort to escape British rule in the Cape. The black Africans in what is now Botswana petitioned Britain for protection. Their request was granted, because the British welcomed allies in the area—their goal was a route north from the Cape to British mines in central Africa.

By the start of the twentieth century, the primarily Dutch and British influx into their territory resulted in the dispossession of the San, causing them to vanish from Natal, many parts of Bechuanaland (now Botswana), and other south-central areas of Africa, just as they had from the Cape Colony.

Slowly but surely, the San's existence was transformed, as much by violence as by the establishment of settled waterholes in their former domain. When droughts came, many San traveled to these waterholes and then chose to continue working for the local farmers rather than return to their traditional life-style. Becoming sedentary and participating in a cash economy instead of bartering as in the past have created great changes and many problems. Even where conditions are good, problems exist.

The Dobi !Kung are a typical example. At the waterhole where they have settled in the Dobe region of Botswana, they have acquired possessions ranging from livestock to beads. These goods make mobility difficult. Cattle and other animals must be fed, gardens must be tended, and beads and other goods could be stolen if not guarded. This is a far cry from the past, when the San could leave their possessions anywhere without worrying about thieves' stealing them.

As a result of having acquired possessions, the San here have more permanent housing, with each home farther apart from others than in the past. They are becoming more and more like their Bantu neighbors, whom they are coming to depend upon to help resolve intratribal differences now that they have too many possessions to allow them to leave the area in cases of disagreements. Marriages of !Kung women to Bantu men are now common. Since the privileges of being a Bantu outweigh those of being a San,

A young San boy tends cattle in modern-day Namibia. Some experts believe that San survival depends upon their ability to become self-sufficient cattle herders.

children of such unions consider themselves more Bantu than San.

Impressed by the material goods of the Bantus and Europeans, the San today consider both groups their superiors. Since the Bantus and Europeans consider the San inferior, the San's low self-appraisal is reinforced.

The San have a tale that reveals their group self-image. In it, the San and Bantu were once one people. Then their creator called for a tug of war, with a rope that had two halves. One half was made of animal skin, the other of grass. The Bantu pulled the animal skin, while the San pulled the grass. The Bantu, pulling the stronger half, won. They received the herds of cattle and other domestic animals, as well as knowledge about farming. The San got only knowledge of the Bush. As one San told John Marshall in the 1950s, if they could have another chance at playing tug-of-war, they would be sure to pull the right half this time.

Change has come to the San in many forms. Herders and farmers have driven larger game animals from some areas. Elsewhere, the cattle are overgrazing the land, so that even if the San wanted to hunt and gather, they have lost much of their customary vegetation as well as their traditional game. More and more, San men are accepting work as cattle herders and other unskilled jobs for which wages are meager, sometimes little more than food, water, and hand-me-down clothing.

San women have their own problems in this changing economy. Since they no longer have plants to gather, they must either work on the farms or become dependent on their husbands. The strong egalitarian relationship that once existed in San families is breaking down, and the woman's place in the community has diminished.

In some areas of Botswana, which became an independent nation in 1966, wealthy British settlers from South Africa have no need of San cattle herders. The San in these towns are unemployed and are considered squatters on their own land. In an effort to help the San support themselves and become integrated into mainstream society, the Botswanan government has inaugurated several projects. It has established resettlement communities, with schools, clinics, waterholes, livestock, and housing. However, the San are finding it difficult to change from being nomadic hunters to pastoral, sedentary farmers. They find the schools hard to get to, the diet unfamiliar, and the life-style unappealing. Add to this their poor self-image and sanitation problems, and the result is a range of pressing problems, including alcoholism and tuberculosis.

Most of the San in Namibia, which was acquired by South Africa after World War I, now live on a reservation set up in 1959. In 1970, the South African government expropriated about 90 percent of the reservation area and gave it to other ethnic groups, thus taking from the Namibian San their means of survival: water and land. On the reservation, the San receive handouts of food, some medical help, and the opportunity to purchase supplies for cash. Hunting animals is no longer practiced, gathering plants has almost completely disappeared, and money has changed the way of life. Instead of depending upon each other as in the past, the San now depend upon the administration and the army of South Africa, which was for a long time the largest single employer of San.

Of the many San who made up the troops, most were recruited in Angola to help the South Africans fight the guerrillas struggling for Namibia's independence. Although their reasons for signing up were economic rather than political, the San became professional soldiers with loyalty to their officers. For these soldiers, army life was a way up, and a chance

—56—

for a bigger paycheck than they could get anywhere else. When Namibia recently won its independence, however, many of the Angolan San soldiers became refugees in Namibia.

Today, the most well-known outsider group helping the San is the !Kung San Foundation, established in Namibia in 1978. The foundation provides funds and material goods as well as basic training in agricultural and herding techniques to !Kung San groups, and has helped at least three of them resettle near traditional waterholes. John Marshall also has a fund to help the San acquire cattle and learn how to herd them so that they can become more self-sufficient.

Those who are most concerned about the San believe that they can only survive culturally and physically if they have economic help as well as a chance to regain a positive sense of their own identity and value. Today, the 50,000 to 60,000 San are not threatened as a race, but their nomadic way of life is almost gone. Once the sole inhabitants of a beautiful African paradise, most no longer have nor want the skills for life as hunter-gatherers. Fathers now want their sons to be educated in order to better themselves. Yet the San as a people lack the political rights to the land they once occupied, as well as the skills to find adequately paid work.

As John Marshall reminds us,

The myth is that there are still people living by hunting and gathering in the Kalahari desert, that people pursue hunting and gathering as a way of life because they want to, that people can survive that way in the world today and it's not so. To ignore the scale and consequences of their extermination and dispossession is like ignoring the Holocaust. The policy was either active extermination or it was dispossession and enslavement.

Filmmaker Jaime Uys recently commented about what it was like to shoot *The Gods Must Be Crazy* in the Kalahari. He said that at first you miss your creature comforts from back home, but by the third day, you are ready to accept that everyone should live this way.[2]

The San, no doubt, feel far more strongly than Uys does about the Kalahari. Whether they can become self-sufficient while retaining their traditional culture and values remains to be seen. Yet, no matter how their future shapes up, John Marshall believes that the San should be remembered not as losers, but as winners. Having known many generations of San, he advises that in thinking about these desert people, we should dwell less on what they are losing than on their admirable ability "to adapt and to survive when all the odds are stacked against them."

BAMBUTI (PYGMIES) of the ITURI FOREST

According to the French geneticist Gerard Lucotte, Adam was an African Pygmy. Dr. Lucotte based his theory on experiments to find a certain genetic material passed down from father to son that leads back to a common paternal ancestor of us all. He found a "master" type of chromosome, then traced it back as far as he could. The result? It was most common in one group: the 300,000 Aka Pygmies of the Central African Republic.[1]

Not all scientists readily accept Lucotte's belief that an African Pygmy is everyone's great-grandfather. However, the possibility is an intriguing introduction to an endangered people who have long fascinated anthropologists.

There are several groups of short-statured people known as Pygmies in the world, but when most people use the word, they are referring to the African Pygmies in central Africa. The "Pygmies" themselves consider that word derogatory and prefer to be known by the name of their specific group. In all, some thirteen different groups of short-statured people—most of whom are no more than 4 feet 8 inches (122 to 142 centimeters) tall—live in central Africa. Those who are the focus of this chapter are collectively known as the Bambuti. They live in the thick Ituri rain forest regions of northeastern Zaire, which was itself known as the Belgian Congo until it became the independent Democratic Republic of the Congo in 1960. In 1971, it was renamed Zaire. Today, Zaire is sprawling, diverse, and the third largest country in Africa.

Almost all of Zaire's people are black Africans, most descended from the Bantu-speaking people who migrated to this area 2,000 to 4,000 years ago. They came from other parts of Africa and found that other black Africans were already living here. These first known inhabitants of what is now Zaire were the Bambuti.

Although scientists are not in agreement about when the Bambuti first began living in the region, we do know that for many centuries they were believed to be no more than a myth. The Greek poet Homer mentioned them in his epic poem the *Iliad*, which many scholars believe was written between 800 and 700 B.C. Later, beginning in the fifteenth century, Portuguese explorers reported that the Pygmies could make themselves invisible. Even today, many people in central Africa fear all Pygmies because they believe the ancient myths that these nomads are tricky and fierce forest dwarfs.

In actuality, the Bambuti are muscular people with widely set-apart eyes and flat noses. They are very much at home in Zaire's moist Ituri forest, where 40,000 of the remaining 150,000 to 200,000

African Pygmies live. They exist here in small and mobile bands with a livelihood based primarily on hunting and gathering combined with trading and some cash exchanges. In fact, their unique trade agreement with the black Bantu agriculturists who live in permanent villages in the Ituri singles them out as much as their short stature. This long-standing, mutually beneficial trade relationship goes back many generations. Most exchanges take place between men who have been exchange partners since they were young, as their fathers were before them. Their sons will be expected to be exchange partners, too. Pairs of villager and Bambuti girls also have a close and lifelong bond. The trade exchanges take several forms.

The villagers count on the Bambuti to help them clear, plant, weed, and harvest their fields. Besides their labor, the Bambuti supply their trade partners with resources from the forest. Colin Turnbull, a famous early chronicler of the Bambuti, fed the myth that the villagers fear the forest. In reality, the Bantu hunt and fish in the forest, sometimes camping along forest rivers for a month at a time. However, the Bambuti do have a special connection with the forest, which they love and respect. To them, the Ituri is everything—their mother and father, the source of all that is good in their existence. They feel intimately bound to this all-encompassing provider of food, clothing, and shelter.

Although the Bantu go into the forest, the Bambuti can supply them with forest riches that they would not get otherwise. The most important forest goods are meat and honey. While the Bambuti are very adept at climbing up to the bee hives high in the

trees, very few Bantu ever climb the trees. They always try to get the Bambuti to do it for them. The Bambuti also take the villagers medicinal plants and the ivory tusks of elephants from the Ituri.

In return, the Bambuti benefit from the trade arrangement in many ways. From the Bantu they receive exchanges in the form of cultivated garden produce, such as bananas and plantains, and maize. Tobacco is considered especially desirable by many Bambuti; in fact, the Efe labor in their Lese villagers' fields primarily in exchange for it, deriving great pleasure from smoking their clay pipes after a long day of hunting. Other trade items they receive from the villagers include salt, soap, cloth, palm oil, starch, metal implements, and clothing. Because the villagers have greater financial power than the Bambuti, they also help provide food for Bambuti rituals and ceremonies, and they assist in organizing these events. Perhaps the villagers' influence on the Bambuti is most often seen at Bambuti marriages. Generally, a Bambuti couple will be wed according to the villagers' customs, and villagers supply the food for a wedding feast. The villagers' ulterior motive is to gain greater control over the Bambuti by having them wed according to village customs.

For as long as anyone in the area can remember, the Bambuti and the villagers have had this mutually

Bambuti children learn to use a bow and arrows in preparation for their future lives as hunters.

— **63** —

satisfying agreement. Each village has a certain group of Bambuti associated with it whom the villagers consider "their Bambuti." When the Bambuti go into the village from the forest, they entertain their hosts with songs and dances, although not the same ones they perform in the forest.

Some of their forest festivals are held to make the forest happy. Known as *molimos*, these festivals are owned by certain families, but others may borrow them. If things go wrong, someone has died, or hunting is scarce, the Bambuti begin a molimo. They reason that the forest is kind to them, so when bad things happen, that must mean that the forest is sleeping. The solution is obvious. Wake up the forest with music—the forest comes alive with the songs the Bambuti men sing each night during a molimo.

In the forest, the Bambuti live in small camps, each consisting of several cone-shaped huts made of saplings covered with leaves. These huts are built around a common space, where a community fire is kept burning. Inside the huts, the Bambuti sleep on beds that are made by lashing sticks together, then using vines to tie them to a frame.

Their dealings with the villagers are usually through one Bambuti spokesman who has been given the role of "chief" by the villagers. But the Bambuti themselves have no formal chiefs or councils. When they return to their forest camp, the village-appointed chief surrenders his authority and no councils take his place. Disputes in the forest are generally resolved by those people in the tribe who are considered to be the best arbitrators. Since age is an influential factor in Bambuti society, arbitrators are usually older men and women. If an area's food resources become depleted, it is also up to the arbi-

In Bambuti camps, cone-shaped huts covered with leaves are arranged in a circle around a central social area.

trators to decide when the group should move and where it should go next.

In traditional Bambuti life, the women play a major economic role yet are exploited in the eyes of anthropologists who have studied them. Women are in charge of the huts and must make sure that they are in good repair. The women are also responsible for gathering the plants, cooking family meals, and helping the men hunt and fish. Child care is their domain, too; the men in Bambuti groups have very little to do with raising children. For women, Bambuti life involves many long hours of hard work.

The men's hardest work is hunting. Bambuti have two main hunting styles, bow and arrow hunting and net hunting. In the north the Efe and Aka are archers; they hunt primarily with a bow and arrows, while the Mbuti and Sua in the south are net hunters, although they too use bows and arrows. In either group, survival depends upon the cooperation of everyone within a band. The worst punishment a Bambuti can receive is to be driven into the forest alone.

Archers use poison arrows, strips of wood that are dipped in poison. The bows and arrow shafts are hardened with fire, the metal arrowpoints sharpened on quartzite. Before the hunt, a group of men start a smoldering fire; its smoke is said to enhance the archers' chances of success magically if they pass their bows and arrows through it.

The bands of Bambuti net hunters are generally larger than those of the archers. Although the net hunters are thought originally to have obtained their nets from their Bantu neighbors, they now make and maintain their own nets, which may be anywhere from 100 to 300 feet (35 to 100 meters) long. A

A Bambuti mother, with her child in tow, works in a villager's garden. In return for her help, she can expect the villager to give her certain products from the garden, as well as other trade items.

A band of Bambuti hunters uses the traditional bow and arrows to hunt their prey deep in the Ituri Forest. Their game is generally distributed to everyone in camp.

common material for nets is nkusu vine, which is knotted and must be kept in good shape; it requires constant inspection for signs of wear and tear. Generally, only married men may own nets.

The night before a net hunt, the men discuss their choices of where and what to hunt until every adult male has spoken and agreement is reached. Then the men dance, imitating the animals they will be seeking the next day. When morning arrives, the hunt is begun with rituals to keep the hunters in harmony with the forest so that it will grant them success.

During a net hunt, the men may arrange as many as thirty nets in a semicircle and tie them to the bushes. Then the hunters conceal themselves behind their nets and the women perform their role. After positioning themselves in a semicircle, facing the nets, they start shouting and beating the brush with sticks. Frightened and confused by the women's noise, the animals rush into the nets. Then the hunters shoot them with arrows or spear them.

Unless the men have killed a large game animal, their catch is taken back to the camp and distributed to everyone, although the exact specifics of sharing the meat vary among Bambuti groups. If a hunt has been good, the food is cooked and eaten after being divided. Then the adults dance, while the story of the hunt is told with song and movement.

The biggest catch is an elephant, although it has been illegal to hunt these animals since the early twentieth century. A band seldom fells more than two elephants a year. Although Bambuti archers generally stay in groups when they hunt elephants, net hunters more often slay elephants singlehandedly, using just a short-handled spear. Like other large game, the elephant must be dissected and distributed where it is caught. The people carry their kettles to the killing site, where they cut up and boil the meat, eating some of it and drying the rest to take to the village as a gift. The tusks go to a villager who will sell them to traders from other countries; the hunter receives a small part of the profit.

To both the villagers and the Bambuti, honey is even more valued than game. While game can be killed throughout the year, honey can only be gathered during a precious small window of time in May and June. During this period, the net hunters, who live in bands of several families, split up into smaller units, and archers, who live in smaller bands, combine into larger units. All the Bambuti—children and adults, men and women—help to gather honey during the honey season, which is a time for special games and dances. At the dances held at the end of each day, the men pretend to gather honey and the women pretend to be bees. But gathering honey is more than fun. It requires great skill at tree climbing, since bee hunters not only have to climb the trees carefully but have to do it while carrying their equipment, including hatchets, torches, and wooden tubes.

Acquiring the skill of tree climbing begins in early childhood. Childhood is also when boys learn how to hunt, using bows and blunt-tipped arrows made from soft wood, and girls practice gathering plants by using small carrying baskets. Both boys and girls may play house; girls build stick and leaf huts, and everyone does adult everyday chores. A sense of community is developed early on; children call everyone in their parents' age group "mother" and "father," while everyone in their own age group is referred to as "brother" or "sister."

Regardless of how the Bambuti may exploit

Exhibiting great skill in tree climbing, this Bambuti man uses vines to help him reach the honey he gathers during the short honey season each year.

their women by encouraging excessive work and engaging in wife beating, they also respect them as the bearers of life. In fact, the most well-known ritual of the Mbuti is the *elima*, held when a girl reaches maturity and has her first menstrual period. The Bambuti rejoice over the significance of a girl's receiving the natural ability to have children, which they consider to be a gift. It calls for a special ceremony that lasts for about a month.[2]

This is a time when a young woman lives in an isolated hut where she is joined by other girls and is watched over by an older female, usually a relative. Inside the elima hut, the young women learn special elima songs that celebrate the blessing of potential motherhood. They are also taught the songs that the women sing and are educated about their duties now that they can bear children. During this time, they must observe certain taboos, such as those restricting the kinds of food they may eat.

In a sense, this ceremony is as much for the young men as it is for the young women. While the initiates are educated inside the hut, eligible young Bambuti bachelors gather outside. When the young women sing their elima songs, the young men answer them. Then the young men wait, hoping for a glimpse of the opposite sex. Every now and then the young women step outside the hut, carrying long whips. If any young man is struck with a whip, he is expected to enter the elima hut. But he proceeds at his own risk since he will have to fight his way in; mock battles that could result in battle scars are part of the ceremony. The battles are a way for the young man to show off his courage.

Once inside, if a young man cares about the young woman who struck him, and if her mother consents, he may lie down beside her and even sleep with her. This is equivalent to becoming engaged. But marriage will not be permitted until the suitor gives the young woman's family a large antelope. As among the Bushmen, this "bride price" is proof that he can take care of a family, and its acceptance means that the couple will be free to marry.

Some elimas take place for only Bambuti girls, others for Bantu and Bambuti girls who go through the ceremony together. This shared experience binds them to each other for life.[3]

Although the elima is as much an initiation for young men as it is for girls, male Bambuti must also go through another ceremony. Known as the *nkumba*, this ceremonial initiation into adult society is held in the villages about every three years. All boys—villagers and Bambuti—between the ages of nine and eleven are expected to take part in this ceremony, which may last for two months or more.

For the villagers, the ceremony marks the boys' transition to adulthood and helps them connect with their past. But the Bambuti go through it only because this is the only way the villagers will acknowledge their maturity. It is not taken as seriously by the Bambuti as it is by the villagers, because the Bambuti have their own legends and connections, which they do not share with the villagers.

The ceremony involves circumcision, during which each boy's sex organ is cut in an operation. The circumcision and the tests of physical endurance that follow it generally take place at an initiation camp. Here, as in the elima hut, the participants must observe various taboos, some restricting what the boys eat, as well as how and with whom they eat. They even have a special bed at this time.

— 73 —

However, after Colin Turnbull shared the campsite with the Bambuti, he reported that they observed the taboos only until their village hosts had departed. Then the Bambuti began eating forbidden foods and dining with whomever they pleased.

When the boys return to the Bambuti camp after the initiation, they are still treated as boys, not men. As evidence of their continued status, they are not allowed to sing the men's molimo songs. Only after a suitor has slain an antelope and taken it to his in-laws is his manhood confirmed.

Here, as in most other tribal groups, there is a strict taboo against marrying a relative. In many camps, this eliminates any possible marriage partner, since everybody is related. That calls for finding a suitable mate from another camp. Generally, when a young man marries, he is expected to take his bride back to his people. He is also expected to find a woman from his camp to replace his bride in her camp, because females are so important to a community's economy. Because men stay in their own natal band and are surrounded by male relatives, while women marry out of their own natal band, it is easy for men to exploit women in Bambuti society.

Bambuti society is unique and it has had impressive staying power. But it is also a society that is threatened today.

CHANGES

Before Zaire became independent in 1960, the Belgian policy in the region was to leave the Bambuti alone. Although some Bambuti and villager groups were forcibly resettled in the 1940s, when the Belgians built roads through the Ituri, by and large the Belgians did not consider the Ituri forest of any great economic value. But during the last few years, the government of Zaire has become more involved in the Ituri's development. More and more areas of the forest are being cut down for roads, mines, and foreign plantations, especially coffee plantations. Each inroad into the forest deprives the Bambuti of still more of their native lands.

In efforts to help the Bambuti, local administrators over the last few years have attempted to "liberate" the Bambuti by setting up villages for them where they could supposedly cultivate their own plantations. Although the intentions seem noble, this has been a disastrous experiment. Leaving their forest homes exposed many Bambuti to alien foods that upset their usual diet. They were also victims of the sun, which was much stronger than they were used to in their canopied forest home. As a result, many Bambuti who moved to the villages suffered severe sunstroke. But perhaps the greatest effect on the history of the Ituri Forest was that of the Simba Rebellion in 1964 to 1965.

The rebellion, which took place during the early days of independence, was staged by poorly organized rebels known as *Simbas*, a Swahili word for rebels. The Simbas entered the Ituri region along the roads built by the Belgians in the 1940s and 1950s. Government forces followed the rebels, and the villagers soon found that their cultivated crops were wanted by both rebels and soldiers. The Bambuti had no choice but to take sides. Some helped their village partners flee into the forest. Others joined the rebels or government soldiers.

After the soldiers had captured the last rebel

leader and the Simba rebellion had officially ended, the Ituri had greatly changed. Forest battles resulted in its former population's being reduced or relocated, and now that government authorities were in the region, they opened the Ituri to new people. Immigrants included wealthy meat traders, gold prospectors, and farmers. Each group was eager to exploit the forest; none was eager to develop a reciprocal trade arrangement with the Bambuti.[4] If the immigrants need help from the Bambuti, they prefer paying them with cash.

The newcomers have had a strong effect on the Bambuti, the villagers, and the Ituri itself. The Bambuti, with no legal rights to the forest, have been forced to watch as all around them trees are being felled to make way for new roads, as well as for settlements and coffee plantations primarily run by European corporations. Each plantation draws migrant workers into the region; these workers are tempted by the promise of both wages and land. The forest is being cleared for the plantations as well as for the migrant workers who labor on them.

Bantu villagers benefit from these plantations. They find work on them, purchase new goods at the plantation store, educate their children at plantation schools, and get medicines from plantation dispensaries. But villagers working at the plantations have little time left to tend their gardens and grow fruits and vegetables to trade with the Bambuti. At the same time, game animals have left areas in which the plantations have been built, so the Bambuti haven't as many forest resources to trade either.

The Bambuti themselves have contributed to the breakdown of their former exchange system.

When wealthy newcomers first migrate to the area, they want the Bambutis' forest resources. Some villagers, such as the Lese (linked with the Efe), complain that the Efe are now trying to get the highest prices they can for their goods rather than honoring their long-term trade agreements. Consequently, the villagers no longer feel they can count on the Efe. Therefore, they offer them less help and the traditional system crumbles even more.

And the Bambuti cannot simply go back to the forest and live without their villagers. While the plantations have displaced game habitats, the meat traders have seriously decimated the game populations. In many areas near the edges of the Ituri, there are no longer any game animals. Bambuti who once lived in these areas either have moved to less populated districts where game remains or have been forced by circumstances to accept work on Bantu farms, on plantations, and, in rare cases, in towns. But wherever they go, Bambuti face prejudice and discrimination, much of it resulting from their lack of education.

Because no jobs exist that accommodate the Bambuti's highly mobile life-style, they are ill equipped for any but the most menial jobs outside the forest. Whether they are working on commercial plantations or in logging operations, as a result of their poor schooling they are paid the lowest wages, as well as receiving the worst housing, limited access to health care, and no priority for educational facilities.

Equally distressing to many Bambuti is the fact that more and more Bambuti women are marrying into the dominant Bantu societies around them.

Consequently, the women are losing their cultural heritage in these unions—they are treated by their husbands as field laborers rather than as essential partners in the economy. As a further indication of the discrimination against the Bambuti, Bantu men can marry Bambuti women, but Bambuti men cannot marry Bantu women.

But Bantu/Bambuti marriages are only a small part of the problem faced by the Bambuti as growing populations continue to press in on all sides of the Ituri to exploit the forest for its game and wood. No matter where we look, the Bambuti's unique hunter-gatherer subsistence culture appears to be threatened.

American anthropologist Dr. Robert Bailey, who has been involved for many years in the Ituri Project to study the Efe and the Lese, reports that the two major concerns now for the Bambuti sound almost contradictory. The first threat is the destruction of the forest, because without the Ituri, the whole culture of the Bambuti will disappear. But the second threat to the Bambuti is conservation! There is now a major attempt to create a huge forest reserve in the Ituri, which is being funded by the World Wildlife Fund, the World Bank, and a number of other conservation agencies. "But they don't know what to do about the people who use the reserve," explains Dr. Bailey. "Should the Pygmies be allowed to continue to use the forest, and if so, what restrictions should be placed on them? In a sense, the European and American communities who are concerned about chimpanzees and elephants and trees are going to decide what Bambuti tradition is and how they can use their land in the traditional way while the rest of the world passes them by." Bailey and others who care about the Bambuti are currently grappling with the issue of what happens to the local people if and when these proposed reserves are built.

According to Dr. Bailey, the Bambuti's biggest problem is that the people who are willing to help them conserve the forest are not willing to recognize that the Bambuti have some right to their own tradition. Because the Bambuti have not been integrated into the political and economic system of the Zaire government, they lack the influence to protect their interests. From what Dr. Bailey can see, the government doesn't know what to do with the Bambuti, and doesn't really consider them citizens.

Bailey and other supporters of the Bambuti have started the Ituri Fund to help them. They have just built a dispensary and trained two Efe tribespeople to become health educators. They are also helping fund a school in the area and will pay the teachers' salaries. Their hope is that schooling can be seasonal, fitting in with the Efe's life-style so that education is available to them when they leave the forest. But, even as the fund and other help are received, Dr. Bailey reminds us that the Bambuti "can only last as long as the forest lasts."

ABORIGINES
— of —

On January 26, 1988, Australia, the sixth largest country in the world, celebrated the 200th anniversary of the landing of the First Fleet. This event commemorated the arrival of Captain Arthur Phillip at Port Jackson in 1788 and the establishment of the first permanent Australian settlement by Europeans. The settlement later became Sydney, Australia's oldest and largest city.

A red letter day? Not to the more than 15,000 Aborigines who gathered in Sydney to protest 200 years of brutality and oppression by the European settlers. To understand the driving force behind the Aborigines' demonstrations, we need to examine the history that led up to that national holiday.

The word *Aborigine* comes from a Latin word meaning "from the beginning." It is used around the globe to designate the first known inhabitants of any region, but it is most commonly applied to the original inhabitants of Australia. Scientists currently believe that today's Aborigines are the descendants of people who first entered the island continent of Australia at least 40,000 years ago.

They are said to have traveled there from southeast Asia at a time when the sea level between Australia and Asia was much lower than it is now. Even so, the trip was impressive, since there was at least 50 miles (80.45 kilometers) of open ocean to cross. Most experts believe that the first Australians traveled in boats of some kind, stepped ashore in northern Australia, and then increased in number as they spread out over the entire country during a span of thousands of years.

Many Aborigines share common physical characteristics, including dark skin, a broad nose, prominent brow ridges, and dark, wavy hair. However, these features can vary greatly, and some Aborigines are fair-skinned and blond.

Traces of Aborigine culture have been found in Australia's dry central deserts, as well as in the northern tropical forests, in the cool southern and eastern woodlands, and along the seacoasts. The Aborigines lived as far south as the island of Tasmania, which is today Australia's smallest state. In this strange new land dominated by tall eucalyptus trees, they learned how to hunt animals and gather the indigenous plants.

Their clothing or lack of it depended on the weather of their region. In the south, where the days were cooler, Aborigines made fur garments from native animals, many of which are found nowhere else in the world. These include many Australian marsupials (mammals that carry their young in pouches on their bellies) such as wallabies and kangaroos, which the Aborigines hunted for their meat

Aborigines, the first Australians, at a temporary camp in Australia's Northern Territory, which many Aborigines consider their spiritual home

and skin for many centuries without making a sizable dent in their total numbers.

Aborigine men made spears of wood, skillfully cutting and carving them with chipped pieces of stone. They used their heavier spears (some weighing as much as 5 pounds [2.28 kg]) primarily for warfare and their lighter spears for hunting trips. In order to give each hurl of the spear extra thrust and range when catching game, they relied on wooden spear throwers, known as *woomeras*. They also used their spears, as well as nets, for fishing. The Aborigines were also skillful at making and using stone tools, including axes and hammers. Among their bone implements were fishhooks and barbs for their spears.

Yet they lacked bows and arrows. Some suggest this absence was a result of Australia's being geographically cut off from the rest of the world by the natural movement of land masses before such tools were invented. However, the Aborigines *are* associated with another fascinating weapon—the boomerang. These flat, curved wooden objects are of two types, returning and nonreturning. Those used for hunting did not return to the thrower, while the returning type was mainly used for playing games.

Aborigine hunters have long been renowned for their great skill at tracking animals. Generation after generation of hunters passed on their secrets to the young, imparting advice about patience as well as such specifics as how to smear one's body with earth so kangaroos would not catch their scent and how to use sign language when hunting together so they could ambush their prey. In the countryside, known as the bush, smaller animals and all plants

Facing page: *This photograph, taken in the early 1960s, shows the boomerang, often used to bring down birds in flight.*
Above: *An Aborigine hunter with a speared wallaby, a small, brightly colored member of the kangaroo family.*

are still cooked over an open fire. Larger animals and fish are cooked in an earth oven which the Aborigines make in a pit in the ground.

Since the men could not always depend on a successful hunt, the women's daily forages for plant foods were crucial to the group's survival. Aborigine women also collected shellfish in shallow water, helped in fish drives, and hunted smaller animals, such as goannas, which are large lizards. They were responsible for cooking all the food as well.

Today, as in the past, the handiest implements for Aborigine women living in the bush are shallow, curved dishes made from bark or wood. These containers, known as *coolamons*, are used for carrying everything from babies to the hundreds of plants they gather. The women also carry food in deep baskets woven of fiber or grass. Often colorfully decorated, these are called dilly bags.

Aborigine women living in the bush today continue to use digging sticks to search for such edibles as root vegetables, edible fungus, birds, eggs, snakes, caterpillars, ants, and small rodents. Another popular food is wild honey, which the Aborigines call "sugerbag." In forested areas, the most important plants are the root vegetables, such as the wild yam or water lily. In the desert, grass seeds are most valuable. These are ground into flour and made into a kind of bread. In more northern regions, breads are made from palm kernels.

Throughout Australia, Aborigines to this day call their food "tucker," and food that comes from the bush is known as bushtucker. And more than food comes from bush plants; other bush products are medicines, brooms, and paints prepared from clays and rocks.

As nomads, the Aborigines formerly possessed a minimum of possessions. No sense weighing themselves down on the trail when everyone could make almost everything he or she needed at the next camp. However, some tribes did excel at making certain items or had easy access to natural resources. For this reason, trade routes existing from coast to coast benefitted all Aborigines. One group might exchange native tobacco for red ochre (from which body paint was made), or another group might trade its stone spearpoints for pearl-shell pendants made by coastal groups. These networks exposed native Australians in different regions to the same culture.

The networks may account for the fact that although the Aborigines speak many different languages—about 500 when outsiders first arrived in the eighteenth century—they have many similarities. Their strongest bond is their spiritual or religious life, with its basis in what the Aborigines call the "Dreamtime." This intriguing word refers to a mystic time long ago when the Ancients—also known as Dreamings or Spirits—created everything that exists on the earth today. These Ancients, whom the Aborigines consider to be their ancestors, are said to have brought the world out of chaos. The trees, rocks, and everything else in the landscape, as well as the sun, the moon, animals, and humans, were all created by the Ancients, who were themselves transformed into the things of the earth. After their deaths, the Ancients are said to have returned to their spiritual state. However, the Aborigines credit them with having left behind a rich legacy of stories and legends that have been incorporated into the Aborigines' spiritual life. According to anthropologist Dr. Aram Yenguyam, an expert on the

Aborigines, their symbolic world is "more rich and complex than any anthropologist has ever been able to understand."

The Ancients also left behind many spiritual laws that the Aborigines value as their greatest possessions. The Aborigines believe that the Ancients made them custodians over their land and gave them a plan for living on it with respect. To them, the land is as much their kin as are the Ancients. The deeds of the Ancients are embedded in sacred sites throughout Australia, many of which have rock paintings that the Aborigines attribute to the Ancients. According to the Aborigines, the sites still possess the power and energy of the Dreamtime.

In the past, these sites were especially important to pregnant Aborigine women because it was traditionally believed that the Ancients had fathered their children. When a woman became pregnant she would determine which spirit was a co-creator by remembering which was associated with a sacred site she had recently passed. This association was crucial since many of her child's religious duties were based on it.

The most revered sacred site for all of the Aborigines is Uluru (commonly known as Ayers Rock) in the desert of central Australia. This huge 1,148-foot (391-meter) tall and 1.5-mile (2.4-kilometer) wide reddish sandstone boulder is a spectacle of exquisite beauty. It goes through magnificent color changes as natural light and shadows transform it daily. The rock itself has many stories about the Ancestors engraved around its base. Other areas of Australia also have rich examples of Aborigine art.

Today, Aborigines of the past are being hailed

Uluru, commonly known as Ayers Rock, is the most important sacred site for the Aborigines. This huge monolith made of sandstone is a tourist attraction today.

for their great creative talent. Many of their cave paintings can still be seen at Australian sites and are now protected as national treasures. The Aborigines also were highly skilled at painting on bark and stone and carving and painting wooden figures. The women's bags and bowls were also works of art, as well as useful implements. As in the past, Aborigines each inherit a Dreaming or Ancestral Being who gives them the privilege of painting its story. The Dreamings exist in great number.

The Aborigines' creative spirit is also revealed in their ceremonies, known as *corroborees*. Still held today, these are often filled with dances, songs, and stories as the Aborigines relive myths from their past. Most corroborees are held at the end of the dry season, some only for men and others only for women. Even in ceremonies that are held for both sexes, the men and women always dance separately. The dances may last for days, and the people often decorate themselves for them. Music is sometimes played on the *didgerido*, a long tubelike instrument made from a bamboo log that termites have partially hollowed out. The didgerido is most typically used in northern Australia.

One of the Aborigines' many stories of the Dreamtime involves the creation of the Southern Cross, the brightest constellation in the Southern Hemisphere. It seems that once, long ago, there lived a man named Mululu who had four daughters he loved greatly.

When Mululu was old and close to death, he called his daughters together. He told them that he would soon go to the home in the sky. However, he did not want them to live on the earth all alone.

This corroboree, the traditional ceremony of the Aborigines, was held to put to rest the spirits of the dead.

Concerned about their welfare, he told them to follow him after he died, which they would be able to do with the help of a great medicine man named Conduk.

After Mululu died, his daughters set out to find Conduk. Following their father's instructions, they traveled for many days until they finally located his camp. When they approached the great man, they were surprised to see that the hairs on his long, thick beard were woven into a giant silver rope. The rope was so long that it extended right up to the sky.

The prospect of climbing such a huge rope frightened the girls, but Conduk assured them that they did not have to worry. Besides, wasn't this the only way they could be reunited with their father? Finally, with Conduk's help and encouragement, one by one they ascended the rope. At the end of it they found their dear father waiting for them.

Today, say the Aborigines, the four daughters are the four bright stars in the Southern Cross. Nearby in the sky is another bright star. We call it Centaurus, but the Aborigines say that it is Mululu. The Southern Cross stars can be seen on Australia's national flag, which also shows the southern Pole Star.

Although other myths are known, most Aborigines have severe restrictions about what legends can be revealed to outsiders. An Aborigine male learns many secrets of his people during his initiation ritual. This usually takes place around the age of ten to twelve, although in some tribes seven-year-olds go through it. The initiation marks the transition from boyhood to manhood and involves many special rites. The elders say that these ceremonies are held to summon the powers of the Ancients so that life will go on in its rightful way.

At this momentous time the boy leaves his family and goes to a special camp just for men and other boys who are being initiated. His mother and other women relatives may wail at his departure, but this is all part of the ritual. The Aborigines believe that the dramatic separation from their mothers is an important part of a male's growing-up process.

Wherever traditions are still observed, a boy may spend as long as a year at the camp. There, he takes part in special corroborees during which older males impersonate ancestors from the Dreamtime and elders chant stories about heroes from that special time. Each boy also endures many physical trials, including circumcision. Circumcision is far more than simply a genital operation for the Aborigines, since many elaborate ceremonies lead up to it and follow it. In some groups, other body markings are also part of the initiation. These may include having a front tooth knocked out or a wooden plug put through the nostrils.

The physical side of the ceremonies is only one aspect of them, for this is also the time when initiates learn respect for the elders' authority and for their own social and kinship obligations. The secrets revealed to each initiate are considered a bond among the males, since they cannot be shared with any of the females or with the younger boys. When the initiates return to the camp as men, a big corroboree is held in their honor. However, the rituals are by no means over. They will continue at intervals for many years to come.

Although the Aborigines' traditional way of life

is simple, their kinship system is quite complex and involves an elaborate structure of relationships by which day-to-day life is governed. Each tribe is generally divided into two "halves," or *moieties*, a division that the Aborigines believe had its origin in the Dreamtime. According to the Aborigine, *all* living things, from insects to humans, belong to one moiety or the other. By social norm, people are supposed to marry into a different moiety than their own. A group in our own country that has this system of moieties is the Ojibwa Indians.

On a smaller scale than the moiety is the Aborigines' tribal divisions into sections some call clans, each of which owns a particular territory. All the clans in a region speak the same language, share the same customs and clan songs, and usually marry among themselves. In most places a child belongs to his or her father's clan and moiety. But in some areas a child belongs to the clan and moiety of his or her mother or that of both parents. Although marriage is usually within the same tribe, it can be across clans; through marriage all of the clans become interrelated.

When a clan welcomes a wife from another group, the new husband's family is obliged to repay his wife's natal clan. Getting married is a simple procedure in the outback—no elaborate wedding

An Aborigine sheepherder
proudly bears the signs
of his initiation
rites on his chest.

hall or lengthy guest lists. The young couple usually just begin living together without any formal ceremony. They often spend their first years together with the wife's family. In some places it is customary for the men to have more than one wife.

In some tribes, special behavior patterns exist, such as certain strict taboos between a man and his wife's mother. The two might not be allowed to say each other's name, to speak to each other, or even to see each other. Such avoidance symbolizes respect rather than a desire to avoid each other.

Like marriage, death is a major life change that the Aborigines handle in traditional ways. In tribes that follow tradition, the body of an Aborigine who has died may be cremated, buried, or raised on a platform of branches. After cremation of a family member in many parts of the Northern Territory, the family stores the bones for months before it holds a final funeral ceremony.

Although a majority of Aborigines live in semi-rural and urban areas today, those who have chosen to remain or return to the bush continue to live in camps that shift according to the seasons and the availability of food in the area. Shelters differ, depending upon the region and the season. They range from fairly solid houses in the southeast to temporary windbreaks of grass in the central desert. In the more tropical northern region, during the rainy season (November to April), the Aborigines create large shelters with curved branches and bark roofing. The roofing traditionally was made from stringybark trees, a kind of eucalyptus. In the dry season (May to October), mosquitoes supersede the rains as the major problem. To combat these pesky insects, shelters are raised on stilts and fires are lit underneath them. The smoke from the fires repels the mosquitoes.

Before intervention by government authorities, the Aborigines lived without kings or presidents, or even a chief of police. Arguments between members of different clans could lead to serious battles, as men used weapons such as decorated war clubs in raids that killed many people. However, within clans, members had a system of cooperation that proved effective in preventing bloodshed. Family members knew that the male head of the family would punish them for being disobedient. Brothers were expected to discipline their sisters, as well as to protect them. When feuds erupted between families, the elders were called upon to settle them. The elders were respected men who were also responsible for carrying on traditions and passing on the group's stories. In the old days, young men aspired to grow into this role, which required many years of instructions from the elders they would someday replace.

CHANGES

For thousands of years, the Aborigines were the only humans to inhabit Australia. In the 1600s, Indonesian fishermen regularly sailed to northern Australia and temporarily camped on the beach before traveling on, but they had little contact with the natives. It was the Europeans who had the greatest impact on changing the Aborigines' life-style forever.

The first known European to land in Australia was a Dutch navigator named Willem Jansz. He briefly visited northeastern Australia in 1606. The famous English explorer Captain James Cook became the first European to reach Australia's east coast when he landed in what would become New South Wales and claimed it for Great Britain in 1770. Eight years later, in 1778, a British fleet of eleven ships, known as the First Fleet, arrived in Australia. Its goal was to relieve overcrowding in British jails by setting up permanent prison colonies in the fertile region Cook had explored.

Prisoners were shipped to the new country, along with prison employees and their families. The Aborigines no longer had Australia to themselves. When the Europeans first arrived, there were approximately 300,000 Aborigines living there. But that number soon declined, mainly from epidemics of imported diseases, including smallpox and tuberculosis, brought by the Europeans.

By the nineteenth century, European settlers were pouring into the country. Sheep herders flocked to the land, finding it excellent for grazing. Later settlers began raising cattle and growing crops such as wheat. The products were shipped back for sale to an eager market in Great Britain. However, while farmers and herders profited from the land, the Aborigines did not. They watched as the new farms and ranches (called stations) caused the wild game to leave traditional hunting grounds. Because the Aborigines had no comprehension of "private property" at that time, they speared the settlers' cattle and sheep for food. Their actions were met with retaliation, and many Aborigines were shot and killed. These violent confrontations, just as the epidemics had, diminished the Aborigine population.

Still more immigrants arrived from Britain when

— **98** —

gold was discovered in Australia in the 1850s. Groups of these newcomers began to establish colonies in various sites. Later, when Australia became independent, each colony became a state. In 1901, they were joined into the Commonwealth of Australia. However, the Aborigines were treated as less than citizens in their own land; they were not allowed to vote until 1962, and the government did not even include them in the national census until 1967.

But long before that their numbers had fallen sharply. The very last full-blooded Tasmanian Aborigine, a woman named Truganini, died in 1876. By 1900 there were only about 66,000 Aborigines left in Australia. And today these original Australians represent only one percent of the country's total population. According to some estimates, of these 160,000 Aborigines only about 50,000 are full blooded. The others are of mixed ancestry—part Aborigine and part European.

In the 1960s, the Aborigines' problems with outsiders to their land came to a head, spurred on by the discovery of enormous mineral deposits in northern Queensland. The most important such deposits are bauxite, from which aluminum is made, and uranium, the largest deposits of which lie underneath Aborigine land. Mining companies received permission from the government to mine these deposits even though they were on Aborigine reserves that had been set up by missionaries in the nineteenth century. Yet the Aborigines did not simply surrender their land, having been inspired in part by the actions American Indians were taking to win their own rights in the United States.

The Aborigines began their struggle for recognition, respect, and rights by first organizing a land rights campaign. As their resistance grew, the government had to begin taking the movement's demands seriously. In 1972, a Department of Aboriginal Affairs was created. Soon afterward, other governmental organizations were formed to work on national land rights legislation.

In 1976, for the first time, the Aborigines were allowed by law to make claims on certain ancient lands in the Northern Territory. Although this was not as broad a land rights program as the native Australians would have wished, it was a major victory.

Land councils were established in the Northern Territory to represent the Aboriginal communities in their dealings with government officials and mining companies, over whose claims the law grants the Aborigines limited veto. In 1981 a national federation of land councils was founded.

In 1985, as part of its effort to protect and preserve areas and objects of special significance to Aborigines, the government returned Uluru (Ayers) Rock to a group of them. The new owners then leased the park back to the government for ninety-nine years so that tourists could visit what has been named Uluru National Park.

Kakadu, another national park in the Northern Territory, was the home of numerous Aborigine groups in the past. It has more than a thousand sites of ancient art, which include symbolic and sacred designs as well as paintings of animals. Kakadu is now protected in part by Aborigine rangers whose training includes classes on how to manage the park as well as lessons about their own heritage. Hotels in the park pay the Aborigines in control an annual fee for use of the land.

Although progress has been made in Aborigine land rights, native Australian leaders are still worried. They know that concessions have been made to mining companies and pastoral groups. They also realize that their peoples' problems are by no means over: the Aborigines remain Australia's most disadvantaged group. According to a 1988 report,[1] Aborigines live an average of twenty years less than other Australians and their infant mortality rate is three times higher than the national average. Furthermore, they are paid far less than white-skinned Australians, even when they hold the same jobs. And although a growing number of Aborigines now hold key government positions, white-skinned Australians still regard the people of the Dreamtime with prejudice. According to Dr. Yenguyam, this prejudice is founded primarily on racism that goes back to nineteenth-century European thought. The Aborigines continue to be looked down upon because of their skin color as well as their culture, which was considered so inferior that Europeans in the past had long debates about whether the Aborigines were even human!

Today, most Aborigines dwell in rural areas in the Northern Territory, Queensland, New South Wales, and Western Australia. Nearly one-third live in poor housing on the fringes of small towns where jobs are few and work is most often found on cattle stations. The prejudice against them results in many problems. As a result of unemployment, families have no money for decent housing, and many people attempt to escape their plight through drinking, which causes additional problems.

On the positive side, however, growing numbers of Aborigines are becoming involved in native-led organizations working peacefully to overcome the problems of the urban fringe-dwelling Aborigines. On their own, some Aborigines are establishing health and legal services. Although their numbers have certainly dwindled from the eighteenth century, when Europeans first arrived on Australia's shores, the Aborigines' strength is growing as their voices get louder in their demands for better education, more land rights, and the chance to preserve their traditional laws.

Other Aborigines have found a solution to their problems by leaving the cities and resettling in remote homelands where they are returning to traditional ways. Most native Australians who still observe their ancient life-style live in the large reserves of the north and center of Australia. There, they try to maintain what they consider to be the most desirable aspects of Aborigine culture: kindness to each other, respect for the elderly, and a relatively peaceful existence.

Today the Aborigines are torn between the desire to become a part of Australia's mainstream society and the strong pull of their social and religious heritage to preserve their time-honored ways. Aborigine customs, from their initiations and mythologies to their kinship ties and everyday values, are strikingly different from the Western ways of the highly industrialized Australia of today.

Increasing respect is being shown throughout the world for the Aborigines' way of life. Their legends are being recorded for posterity, and their artistic expression is receiving vast acclaim. Their

The past and present merge as a contemporary Aborigine uses a shortwave radio powered by solar batteries to call his relatives to a ceremonial cycle.

continuous tradition of visual art is acknowledged as the oldest on the earth. Although Aborigine artists stopped painting on rocks about eighteen years ago, their contemporary paintings on bark, as well as on canvas, are becoming world-famous.[2] One difference from the past is that today's painters are as likely to be women as men, whereas in the past only men could paint. Far away from Australia, in the metropolitan art center of New York City, the Australia Gallery specializes in Aborigine art. In urban centers worldwide, art connoisseurs are buying paintings that for the Aborigine artist are ways to be joined with the Dreamtime.

Yet the progress being made is not rapid enough for many Aborigines, especially the elders. They worry about the future of their culture as they observe Aborigine youngsters' turning their backs on the old ways. The elders wonder who will pass on their stories and preserve their rituals. Just as disconcerting is their fear that if the old ways they have so carefully nurtured are not preserved, the life force will be broken and great retribution will follow.[3]

INUITS (ESKIMOS) of the ARCTIC

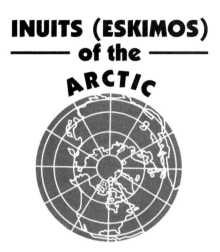

William H. Seward was the United States secretary of state who negotiated the United States's purchase of Alaska from Russia in 1867. Shortly afterward, speaking of the Eskimos (Inuits), he said, "We shall more deeply regret than ever before that a people so gifted by nature, so vigorous and energetic . . . can neither be preserved as a distinct social community nor incorporated into our society."

Today, Seward's words seem more prophetic than ever as we examine what has happened throughout the Eskimos' homeland since their land was first explored, settled, and exploited by outsiders.

The word *Eskimo* is derived from an Algonquian Indian word that means "eaters of raw meat," which the Eskimos were and which made the Algonquians think them strange. However, the Eskimos call themselves the Inuit, Inupiat, Yupik, or Kalatdlit, depending on which region they're from. All of these words mean "the real people," and out of respect the word *Inuit* is used to refer to all the real people in this chapter.

The Inuit's homeland extends over some million square miles throughout Arctic Canada, as well as Greenland, Alaska, and the northeastern tip of Siberia. Their land includes mainland regions as well as islands in the Bering Sea and many northern Canadian islands.

While their total population of approximately 110,000 people is thinly distributed today, most Inuits live in towns and small communities along the coastlines. They have settled primarily where food is plentiful and animals can still be hunted for subsistence or as a supplement to a paying job.

The Inuits speak two main languages: Yupik in the southern part of Alaska and in Siberia and Inupik (Inupiaq) elsewhere. All the Inuits share the physical similarity of stocky builds, wide faces with high cheekbones, straight black hair and dark eyes, and light brown skin color. In many ways they resemble the Siberian people of northern Asia: they have the same narrow slanting eyelids with an inner eyefold known as an epicanthal fold. This is explained by the fact that, like American Indians, the Inuits' prehistoric ancestors lived in Siberia. They entered Alaska perhaps 8,000 years ago, traveling across a temporary frozen bridge of water over the Bering Strait.

From Alaska, the Inuits' ancestors journeyed eastward, reaching Greenland by perhaps A.D. 1200. Experts believe that there were two migratory waves of pre-Inuits. The first, known as the Dorset culture, dominated the region for some two thousand years. The Dorsets are believed to have in-

—106—

This photograph, taken at the turn of the century in Port Clarence, Alaska, shows an Inuit group wearing their traditional fur parkas.

vented the snow houses known as igloos. By A.D. 1000, a second migration, known as the Thules, had replaced the Dorset people. More settled than the Dorsets, the Thules are considered to be the true ancestors of the modern Inuits living in Greenland, Canada, and northeastern Alaska. Separate Inuit groups, each differing at least slightly in life-style, traditions, and history from the others, live in these different countries. However, the groups share enough similarities for us to consider the Inuits as one entity.

If one word could be used to epitomize the Inuits among the world's cultures, it would have to be "resourceful." Here are people who have managed to survive for many centuries in the harshest, coldest region on earth. Their history is evidence of their perseverance and self-reliance.

The long, cold winters and short, cool summers of the far north were instrumental in shaping how they lived. The land is mainly tundra, a frozen surface with water underneath. Forests cannot grow here, although the minisummer comes alive with colorful wildflowers joining the more sedate lichens, mosses, and shrubs. Plants in this remote region are rarely eaten, since the vegetation is not abundant, easily digested, or tasty.

In the past, when desirable vegetable resources were sparse at best, the Inuit mainly ate meat and fish. Much of their food was from the sea, including many sea mammals such as seals, walruses, narwhales, and whales. Although sea mammals are both difficult and dangerous to hunt, during certain seasons they were the only source of food. They were also important sources of clothing and oil, which provided light, heat, and medicine. For the traditional Inuit of today, hunting sea mammals continues to call for great patience, endurance, and skill, as well as spiritual assistance so that each hunt will be successful. The latter requires hunters to have a spiritual framework for their lives. At the same time, the real world presents very real problems to these primarily coastal people.

While other groups who rely on food from the sea can simply spear their catch, the Inuit have had to find a way to prevent their huge catch from sinking when speared. Their solution was to develop harpoons: spears with a detachable head or barb made from the tips of walrus tusks and joined to the spear by a line. When a harpoon head enters an animal's body it detaches from the shaft and turns beneath the skin so that it cannot come out easily. The hunter can then prevent the animal from sinking by attaching the other end of the line to something that can weigh it down, such as a seal bladder, or by holding the line himself.

The most sought-after sea mammal is the seal. Seal hunting techniques vary, depending on the season. When most of the larger sea mammals migrate south in the winter, seals are the only sea mammals available. With much of the Inuits' region frozen over, winter seal hunting is best done from the holes seals make in the ice when they come up for air.

Hunters use their dogs, which we call huskies, to sniff out seal breathing holes beneath the snow. When a hole is found, the hunter stations himself at it for a wait that might last for days. For protection and comfort, he builds a windbreak of snow blocks and a snow-block seat. Then he sticks a thin, pointed

rod of stone into the snow until it reaches the water. When the stick wiggles, he knows that a seal is at the hole. Quickly he thrusts his harpoon into the hole to get his prey. Then he digs away the snow and drags the seal up. One hunter might wait alone, or several hunters may congregate next to a large hole. That way, an entire herd of seals can be harpooned at once when they surface.

In the spring, when the seals come out onto the ice to bask in the sun, the hunters kill them as they sleep. This calls for great skill in sneaking up on the seals. In some regions, hunters use seal claws to imitate seal sounds. When the hunter is within striking distance, he stuns the seal with his harpoon, then finishes the job with his knife.

In the late spring and summer, when the ice had melted, the Inuits hunted seals from lightweight boats called *kayaks*. Today kayaks are found only in Greenland. Most kayaks have a wooden or bone frame covered with sealskin, and a hole in the top large enough for one man to sit in. Some kayaks have two holes and can carry two men. Considered some of the most efficient hunting boats ever invented,

Top: *The traditional Inuit of today hunts sea mammals, using modern equipment and centuries-old strategies.* Bottom: *By using the harpoon, the Inuits can retrieve their prey at sea, rather than have it sink to the bottom of the water.*

kayaks are maneuvered with one or more paddles. When an Inuit hunter uses a kayak, he becomes one with it. The hunter usually wears a waterproof jacket—made of seal intestine in the old days—that can be wrapped so that he fits snugly in the hole. Should his boat flip over, the paddler can roll back up and keep afloat.

Another kind of boat used by the Inuits, known as an *umiak*, is found today in only a few Alaskan villages. This vessel has a wooden frame and a waterproof cover made from several large seals or walruses. It can hold up to twelve people and, like the kayak, is propelled by paddles.

In parts of the Eastern Arctic, groups of men in individual kayaks hunted larger sea animals together. Elsewhere, umiaks were used to hunt walruses and whales. Whales, sought in the summer, were especially valued because they could weigh up to 60 tons and had as much blubber, or fat, as 1,000 seals. Blubber was especially useful for fueling lamps. Today, as was true a thousand years ago, it takes much teamwork to haul in a whale. Friends, neighbors, and relatives join together to move the whale from the water to solid ice. But the event isn't strictly work; butchering begins at once, and the people share in a feast at the butchering site before they take home a share of the meat and *muktuk*, the black skin lined with blubber.

This one-man kayak almost becomes a part of the hunter's body.

On land, today's most important game animal continues to be the caribou, or wild North American reindeer, whose meat is preferred to seal meat. In the past, the caribou were important for everything from food and clothing to housing, oil, and tools. They also served as a source of respect and spiritual guidance for the people. Everyone, from children to elders, was involved in the harvest of these creatures, and the hunt helped to unify the people and educate them about life.

Hunting caribou requires great skill as well as luck, since these migratory animals have unpredictable routes. Even so, hunters have to try to predict the herd's movements for each new summer/fall hunting season and then hope they can head off the herd and ambush the animals. Caribou are hunted after herds have journeyed north from the woodlands to find food and to give birth. The women and children usually drive the animals toward the men, who finish the job with spears, bows and arrows, or more currently, rifles.

Before the introduction of guns, Inuit hunters relied exclusively upon their excellent hunting kits. These featured a variety of arrows, spears, or harpoons—just the right weapon for each particular type of mammal, fish, or bird they were stalking. Survival in their homeland called for proficiency in killing animals such as musk oxen, beavers, foxes, and rabbits. Polar bears were considered too dangerous to pursue, but hunters were usually prepared to try taking them if they were encountered by accident. Among the birds the Inuit hunt are ptarmigans, murres, and waterfowl. Especially in Alaska, fish is another important food source. Today, as in the past,

For the Inuit, caribou are as much a source of spiritual guidance as a source of food and clothing. Here, caribou are being prepared for the market.

the most common Arctic fish is the char, a type of trout. Like the salmon, char are caught primarily during their annual summer migration from the sea into fresh water.

In the old days, the Eastern Inuits generally caught fish with the help of a weir or a leister spear. A weir is a wall of stones or wood built across a shallow stream; leister spears have two barbed prongs on each side and a shorter prong in the center. In the Western Arctic, the Inuit used fishing nets made from materials such as sealskin, shredded whalebone, and shredded willow bark. The women made these nets and often tied their individual nets together into one large communal net.

Sometimes the Inuit cooked their meat over the smokeless clay or lamps they invented. Resourceful, they found solutions to the most difficult problems. Since there was usually no wood for a fire, they burned seal oil or whale oil if they had it. No oil from sea mammals? They used fish oil instead. No fish oil? Then raw meat would have to do.

Outsiders learned from the Inuits' ways and imitated their clothing. Traditionally, Inuit women made clothes for their family from animal skins tailored so the seams were waterproof. Caribou was the favored skin, especially for winter, since it was warm yet lightweight. Other skins used were those of seals, polar bears, and foxes. Everyone wore the same basic outfit: a hooded parka, trousers, mittens, socks, and knee-high boots called *mukluks*. An important accessory for many Inuits was a pair of goggles with fine slits in it. Made of wood, bone, or ivory, these helped reduce the glare of sunlight on the snow.

Two Inuit women of the Western Arctic use fish nets under the ice to catch fish in the dead of winter.

For many decades, the main point school-children who studied the Inuits remembered was that they lived in snow houses called *igloos*. Today we realize that their igloos were not as widespread as was once believed. Actually, the word *igloo* comes from the Inuit word *iglu* and is used to mean all houses, not just those made of snow.

As a migratory people, most Inuits had a summer home and a winter home. Summer dwellings were usually sealskin or caribou skin tents. The basic Inuit winter home was made of sod (turf) over a framework of wood or whalebone. Built partially below level ground, most sod houses had an entrance tunnel which doubled as storage space and led into a living space.

The snow houses, or igloos, associated with the Inuits were used as permanent winter homes only by Inuits in central Canada and the northern Canadian islands. Elsewhere, snow houses were only temporary shelters for travelers. In rare instances, some are still constructed by Arctic travelers today. Made of hardened, wind-packed snow, these ingenious

Top: *Schoolchildren in modern-day Canada build the traditional Inuit igloo in an igloo-building contest.*
Bottom: *In contrast to the snow houses known as igloos, this temporary summer home is constructed of sealskin or caribou skins.*

dome-shaped structures can be strong enough to withstand violent winds. They can also be quite comfortable, because snow has tiny pockets that trap air, making it an excellent insulating material that keeps the warmth in and the cold out.

In the old days, the Inuits built their snow houses with long straight knives made of bone until iron became available when Europeans arrived. Using the knives, the Inuits cut out blocks of ice that were fairly easy to extract once the weather had hardened them. Generally one man worked from the inside, fitting the blocks together in an ascending spiral shape. A companion helped from the outside. When the man inside was finished, he let himself out of his new home by cutting a doorway in his wall of snow blocks. A simple snow house could require about thirty to forty snow blocks to complete and could be built by one or two skilled people in a few hours. Speed was of the essence, because the houses often had to be erected when light was limited and strong winds and extreme cold made any outdoor activity extremely difficult. The art of building a snow house took years to learn.

While an occasional traveler may build a small snow house today, those of the past were far more elaborate structures, often with a wind-breaking entrance tunnel that had storerooms and led to a larger room. There, the heat from seal-oil lamps helped to keep the temperature comfortable for the inhabitants. The lamp also provided heat and light and acted as a clothes drier and a stove.

Traditionally, these amazing snow dwellings had separate areas for cooking, living, and sleeping. A bench of snow built all around the inside was covered with animal skin to serve as a table, seat, and comfortable bed. Eventually, when the snow house's walls turned to ice, the structure became too cold and moist to inhabit. At that point, a new snow house was built and the old one was abandoned.

The Inuits' land transportation, like their homes, was ingeniously matched to their snowy environment. Before snowmobiles revolutionized overground travel, they used sleds pulled by huskies; the huskies were fitted with boots to protect their feet from the ice. Wood was the preferred material for the sleds, but if that was unavailable, the Inuits used whale jawbones or frozen animal skins (seal skins could be soaked in water, then wrapped around several split fish and set out in the cold to freeze into a solid shape).

As one might imagine, in a world where life was often difficult, cooperation was critical. Food and most other belongings were shared by all, and everyone tried to live at peace with everyone else. If an individual didn't get help during a poor hunting season or while building a house during a roaring blizzard, death could be the consequence. Maintaining good relations was in everyone's best interest. Groups varied in size from one family to several hundred persons, depending on the season and the type of hunting being done. In northern Alaska, Inuits gathered together in large groups mainly during the summer and fall when they tracked caribou. In northern Canada, the largest groups of Inuits came together in the winter to hunt seals.

Although the Pacific Inuits had hereditary village chiefs, elsewhere the Inuits had no community officials. The closest they came to leaders was in

Alaska, where whale hunters generally had a captain on each larger umiak. Otherwise, the male head of each family usually had the most authority in it. However, someone with good logic and special abilities might have a wider influence than just over his immediate family. This was especially true of elders, who might be called upon by other community members to judge someone who had committed a serious crime such as murder. Lesser disagreements might be resolved with wrestling matches as well as song duels in which two people tried to outdo each other with insults and ridicule. Both wrestling matches and song duels were performed before an audience. The object was to keep the group intact. However, when interpersonal problems proved unresolvable, the family group often divided, or the feuding person in it left with his or her family to join another group of relatives.

In the past, the Inuits lived in extended families consisting of a husband and wife, their unmarried children, and their married sons' families. These families would share one structure or live in several nearby houses. Although there were no wedding ceremonies, marriage was an important part of an Inuit's life. Most couples were considered married when the man and woman started living together. In some groups, such as the Caribou Inuits, parents chose their offspring's future marriage partners in early childhood.

The roles of men and women were well defined. Men built the igloos; made weapons, tools and utensils, kayaks and sleds; hunted for food; tended the dogs; and provided for the elderly and any needy neighbors. The woman was the center of the household, caring for the children, cooking the food, adding fuel to the oil lamps, and making and repairing the clothes. Women also helped build homes and even hunted on occasion.

It was not unusual for a rich man to have two or more wives if he could support them, along with all their children and his wives' parents. In some areas, there were unions of two men and one woman, but this was rare. Another Inuit marriage practice was "co-marriage," in which two couples temporarily exchanged sexual partners. This set up mutual obligations of sharing, protection, and support that lasted for many generations since all the offspring considered themselves related.

But no matter what kind of relationships families had, the communities were close-knit. In each one, elders were respected for their wisdom and passed on their knowledge to younger group members. Children were also highly valued, since the future of the community rested with them. In the past, as today, one of the greatest bonds among the Inuits is their shared spiritual beliefs. Even where Christianity has become the main religion, beliefs from the past are incorporated in the Inuits' lifeways.

Their world is governed by many taboos and rituals, most of which they traditionally follow to win favor with the powerful spirits that control nature. Inuits believe that people and other animals have souls that live in another world after death. They try not to offend these spirits and souls, fearing punishment if they do. Like many other tribal people, the Inuits believe that game animals are not so much killed as allow themselves to be taken. Such thinking gives every hunt a spiritual context and binds the hunter to the hunted in a special way.

One of the most important spirits for the Inuits is

Sedna, the Spirit of the Sea, a goddess who lives underwater. The Inuits fear that if they displease Sedna, she will send the animals away so that the hunters will be hungry. To keep Sedna happy, the Inuits have many rules and taboos regarding sea animals. In parts of Alaska they save the bladders of the seals they kill each year. Then, on the last day of the annual six-day Bladder Festival in December, they throw the bladders into the sea so that they can be reborn as seals in the spring.

Among the Eastern Inuits, festivals were held in the past whenever people assembled with enough food to go around. In the old days, Western Inuits held equally casual gatherings. They also had more formal festivals throughout the year. The most elaborate of all were those celebrations held by the Inuits in western Alaska.

As in the past, the shamans or *angakkoqs* play a central role in most of the Inuit festivals. They reportedly have great ability to communicate with spirits and bargain with them to bring good luck, as well as to cure illness and foresee the future. Shamans are believed able to go into a trance and leave their bodies behind to visit Sedna beneath the sea. There they will plead their people's case to her. Some shamans receive their power in mystical ways. Others seek it out and apprentice themselves to practicing shamans.

Another source of supernatural power is found in charms, which people carry with them to improve their fate. Charms may range from birds' claws and beaks to dried flowers, ivory carvings, and pieces of stone. Besides being sewn into clothing, personal charms can be worn on a string necklace or carried in a pouch. They are also designed into the handles of tools or weapons. Charms may be found by accident, given to people, or sold to them by a shaman. Once someone receives a charm, it is passed on from one generation to another. Spells, which are words that have a magical effect and are sung or spoken, are another source of supernatural power. Like charms, spells are usually given to someone or bought from a shaman.

For the Inuits, names also have power. In the past, a baby was not considered human until he or she was named. In some places, name giving was treated casually, while in other regions, such as Southwest Alaska, it called for a special ceremony. Here, a name was considered so sacred that once it was given it could no longer be used in everyday life. Instead, people called children by nicknames. They also treated them with the same respect given the deceased person for whom the child was named, since the child was thought to have that person's soul.

At the other end of the spectrum, death for the Inuits is simply a continuation of the life cycle because they believe that while the flesh will decompose, the soul will eventually be reborn in another human form. In the past in most regions the deceased's body was wrapped in animal skins and laid on the ground, a circle of stones around it. Inuits placed tools and other useful items beside the body so the soul would have them in the next world until it was reborn into a new baby.

Perhaps it is the Inuits' centuries-old belief in a world filled with spirits and souls that has made their artistic expression manifest in many gracefully created everyday items. They have managed to fashion ivory, bone, caribou antler, skins, and fur into works

of art that are collectors' items today. Their creativity is also revealed in the many games, stories, and dances with which they passed away the long winter nights.

CHANGES

The first Europeans to encounter Inuits were the Vikings, who were living in Greenland when Inuits arrived there about A.D. 1100. Later, during the late 1500s, European explorers met Inuits in the eastern regions of Arctic North America. But it wasn't until the eighteenth century that Russians and other Europeans "discovered" Alaskan Inuits.

Soon, large numbers of European whalers and fur traders were pouring into Inuit regions. Whalers were particularly interested in whalebone, from which corsets were made. These outsiders not only hired Inuits to work for them but traded with them. The newcomers were especially eager to acquire the Inuits' animal skins and ivory. In return, the Inuits received a variety of valued trade goods including rifles, ammunition, iron, wood, and cloth, all of which had a profound impact on their way of life, bringing about changes in everything from their hunting techniques to their everyday cooking.

One of many fine contemporary artists, Mary Pudlap works on a drawing at a print cooperative in Canada.

Tragically, the newcomers also brought many diseases against which the Inuits had little resistance. In a sad, but familiar story, many natives soon died from measles, smallpox, and other diseases of epidemic proportions. The newcomers also brought alcohol, which has become a major problem for the Inuits. Like other people throughout the world, many Inuits have turned to the bottle as an escape from their other problems, only to find that alcohol becomes a major problem in itself.

By the time a depletion in the available whales caused the whaling industry to collapse in the early 1900s, the fur trade was booming. Many Inuits started trapping animals, especially foxes, for the fur traders. As contact between the Inuits and non-Inuits increased, cash began to replace old-fashioned community cooperation and the Inuits' way of life underwent great transformations.

The missionaries who entered the territory, hoping to convert the Inuits to Christianity, contributed to the rapid changes. They challenged traditions by insisting that men have only one wife, and shamans no longer perform their rituals. They sent Inuit children away to mission schools, where native customs and language were not part of the curriculum. The gap between generations broadened as children returned home and found that they could no longer communicate with their grandparents and learn from their ways.

After World War II, improved medical aid helped bring about an increase in Inuit family populations. At the same time, the greater numbers of hunters, fur traders, and whalers in Inuit regions led to a depletion of many land and sea animals. Consequently, many Inuits became unable to support their growing families adequately. More and more, they had to abandon their traditional life-style and seek employment from outsiders who had settled in their areas.

By the 1950s and 1960s, with populations rising and hunting resources and traditional skills declining, disease, starvation, and alcoholism became rampant among the Inuits, especially in North America. These natives were caught in a familiar vicious cycle: because jobs were few, they had little money to support their families; as their self-esteem fell, and their welfare suffered, they became susceptible to many ills of society. They were finding it very hard to do what was being asked of them: make a giant leap from the Stone Age to the Modern Age in the span of just a few decades.

The governments of the various countries where the Inuits lived each attempted to help by moving them many miles from their homelands into permanent communities with schools, hospitals, and other facilities. Even with the best of intentions, this was not always a good solution. In the North's growing cities, Inuits found it difficult for families to live near each other as they had in the past. Family life became fragmented, adding to the daily despair. As mentioned earlier, with few jobs available, many Inuits turned to alcohol; others committed suicide or returned to their original homes.

In the twentieth century, the Inuits' history and present situation differ depending upon the region being considered. Basically, Inuits in Greenland and Siberia have been much more successful in preserving their life-style than those in North America.

In Siberia, after the Communist government took control of all Inuit communities during the 1920s, it began improving the health care, housing, and education available to them. By then, fur traders had already devastated the Inuit population by the introduction of diseases that resulted in deadly epidemics. Soviet education, by turning its back on the traditional language and culture, threatened the Inuit life-style. But the Soviets also boosted the Inuit economy by encouraging them to make and sell items such as reindeer hides and bone and soapstone carvings. These were made available to other parts of the Soviet Union.

Today, about 1,500 Inuits still live on the northeastern tip of Siberia, where they herd reindeer, hunt walruses and other animals, and sell their handicrafts. Meanwhile, the Soviet government has assisted them with education, housing, and other benefits. No doubt the recent break-up of the Soviet Union will affect the Siberian Inuits, as it will all citizens of that republic.

In Greenland, as a result of a warming trend, seals that were once caught in the country's coastal waters were driven farther away. Consequently, by the early 1900s many Inuits changed from seal hunting to commercial fishing. Also around this time, the Danish government, which made Greenland a colony in 1380, initiated programs to improve the Inuits' housing, health care, and education. But education focused on the Danish language and culture, causing Inuit family ties to weaken.

In 1953, the Inuits were made Danish citizens when Denmark changed Greenland's status to that of a province, with equal rights with the rest of the

Danish kingdom. In 1979, Greenland gained home rule; Denmark's constitution is effective in it, but Greenland has its own government for internal affairs. Today, about 42,000 Inuits, most of mixed Inuit and European ancestry, make up the majority of Greenland's population. Although most Inuits here are employed in the commercial fishing industry, those in northern Greenland can still subsist on seal hunting and are able to keep many traditional customs. The government is helping to train them for jobs in various fields.

In Canada, outsiders began arriving in the nineteenth century, hungry for furs, gold, silver, and other riches. In the 1920s, oil and gas discoveries brought more non-Inuits pouring into Inuit territory. However, it wasn't until the 1950s that the Inuits' way of life began changing at a rapid pace. By then, the caribou herds were sharply depleted, as was the fur trade, prompting many Canadian Inuits to relocate to stable communities. They moved near trading posts, mission churches, and government offices where they hoped to find work. But permanent employment continues to be limited, and joblessness is still taking its toll both physically and mentally. So, too, does an educational system that separates children from their parents, producing breaks in families.

Today, about 25,000 Inuits live in Canada, most in small towns where they receive financial and other aid from the Canadian government. The government also has helped the Inuits set up their own fishing and handicraft cooperatives. But many problems clearly remain; the suicide rate among Canadian Inuits is several times higher than Canada's national average. Equally revealing is the fact that in 1986 only one in eight Inuits held a full-time year-round job.[1]

However, there is also hopeful news from Canada—the Canadian Inuits have become increasingly vocal about their cause. They realize that they no longer have the option of turning their backs on the world of today and returning totally to their traditional life-style. Instead, they are fighting to control the mineral wealth produced from their land. Two Canadian Inuit organizations have formed to negotiate with the government. These are the Committee for Original People's Entitlement (COPE), which represents the Inuits of the western Arctic region, and the Inuit Tapirisat of Canada, the national association of Inuits. In 1991, the Canadian government and the Inuits of the Northwest Territories reached a tentative agreement that will give the Inuits control over 740,000 square miles (1,916,600 sq km) of land—an area three times the size of Texas. The land, which is the eastern half of the Northwest Territories, will be called Nunavit, an Inuit word that means "homeland." In exchange for the land and a monetary compensation, the Inuits are to surrender their claim to the rest of the Northwest Territories, where they have lived for thousands of years.

In Alaska, widespread trapping and hunting with rifles had massively reduced the population of most larger game animals by the early 1900s. Disease also took its toll, as half of the Alaskan Inuit population died between 1888 and 1908. The government tried to improve matters by importing reindeer from Siberia for them to herd. This was never a successful venture, because the Inuits were not interested in herding and had no traditional understanding of it. Nor is their area appropriate for managing animals in herds, which require vast grazing lands.

During World War II (1939–1945), many Inuits left their homelands and herds to work at United States military posts in Alaska. After the war, when the posts were dismantled, joblessness became widespread among the Inuits, forcing many to accept temporary work in enterprises started by the newcomers then streaming into Alaska. These included fishing and construction ventures. But unemployment and its attendant problems remain for the Alaskan Inuits, and the United States government has set up many programs to improve their living conditions.

At the same time, big businesses, enticed by the mineral riches buried beneath the land, continue their struggle to gain possession of Inuit homelands and hunting grounds. The most recent controversy is over the possible development of the Arctic National Wildlife Refuge area for its rich oil reserves. Since this is also land where caribou graze, the Inuit are protesting its development on several grounds. They consider the land sacred because of the educational and spiritual lessons they have learned on it. On a more practical note, they worry that the development will force the caribou to leave, taking with them an entire way of life. The Inuit also oppose the development because of the fragility of the land: things grow and decompose so slowly here that any pollution in the water or toxins in the air will overburden nature for a long, long time.[2]

Today, Alaska has about 30,000 Inuits, including some 6,000 Aleuts, a group of Inuits who live on Alaska's Aleutian Islands and on the Alaskan Peninsula. The majority of Alaska's Inuits dwell in small settlements where they struggle to combine a cash economy with hunting and gathering most of their food. Seals, birds, and caribou are hunted year round. In the summer or fall, usually one or two whales are taken, as the International Whaling Commission sets whale quotas for each Alaskan whaling village. But many Alaskan Inuits are unemployed or are employed only marginally, and the United States government provides aid to them in many ways.

A unique situation exists here because the Alaska Federation of Natives (AFN), founded in 1966 by Inuits and American Indians, was able to negotiate in 1971 with the United States government for land rights. This plan was made possible because oil was struck on Alaska's North Slope in 1968, and the government wanted access to Alaska's hidden riches. The final agreement awarded about 40 million acres (16 million hectares) of Alaskan land and nearly 500 million dollars to the state's native people. In return, the natives relinquished their claims to the rest of Alaskan lands.

The land was divided into thirteen regional corporations, which in turn were divided into village corporations. Each person with one-quarter or more Alaskan Native blood received 100 shares of stock in a village corporation and 100 shares in a regional corporation. Originally the shares were not to be sold until 1991, but in that year, at the request of the Alaskan Federation of Natives, the restrictions on selling stocks were extended until mid-1993.

Unfortunately, the program has not been highly successful in many Inuit communities, often because of inexperience or poor management of funds. In 1989, Alaskan Inuits and Indians were still almost twice as poor as other Alaskans.[3] In areas where oil discoveries have been most pronounced, living conditions for the Inuits have improved most.

Wainwright, Alaska, is located on the North Slope, where oil was first discovered in 1968. If you had visited Wainwright in 1968 and then returned to the area today, you would be amazed to see that nothing in the town has remained the same. In 1968 there was not a single automobile in Wainwright. Today, the streets are filled with trucks and cars. In 1968 schools were small and had little equipment. Today they are very modern, with well-equipped science laboratories. Here, as elsewhere in Alaska, few people use a seal oil lamp anymore; wooden homes have replaced yesteryear's sod homes and they are made toasty warm by oil-burning stoves.

These days, even citizens in many remote Alaskan regions can flip the channels and watch the latest television shows beamed from satellites. If they have the cash to buy them, they can wear stylish down parkas purchased from the store rather than their homemade winter garments. Motorboats now take them across the water, and snowmobiles zip them through the snow, while their huskies are now reserved for races. These trappings of modern life call for cash, which is not always easy to come by. Some Inuits pay to be part of the American dream of affluence by working for the government, the oil companies, fish canneries, and other private enterprises. Yet the majority today do not complete high school, despite the many educational programs set up by the government for their behalf.

At the same time, the Inuits' changing diet has

— 135 —

meant that heart disease, once unknown to them, is now a major problem. And where unemployment among them is high, child beating and spouse beating, also formerly unknown, have become commonplace. Yet the world population of Inuits has grown steadily between 1950 and 1970, so that the people are considered to be endangered culturally much more than physically.

But while Inuit dances in more modern Alaskan cities are now being done with modern Michael Jackson moves and few can perform the ancient festivals that once united individuals with the invisible world around them, there is also a growing movement among younger Inuits to find new pride in their culture. In population pockets throughout Alaska, this pride is manifested by younger people who try to record the stories of the elders, reinstate traditional sporting competitions, take their families on traditional hunting and fishing trips on weekends, and revive ancient ceremonies.

Perhaps the most promising news for the Inuits comes from the political arena. In 1977, the Inuits who live below the Arctic Circle in Alaska, Canada, and Greenland organized the Inuit Circumpolar Conference (ICC). In so doing, the group acknowledged its awareness of a heritage shared by all peoples of the Circumpolar region. The ICC, which now represents 130,000 Inuits, has nongovernmental organization status at the United Nations. In 1987, representatives of the Soviet Inuits attended a meeting of the ICC for the first time.

The main goal of the ICC is to protect Inuit land rights, culture, and language as well as the animal life and ecology of their environment. It is attempting to influence the governments of the United States, Canada, and Greenland in issues that range from culture and education to nuclear testing and uranium mining. Within the ICC, Inuit elders have organized their own group, dedicated to passing on knowledge to younger members.

Just as the Inuit adapted to the harsh realities of the Arctic region, they may well be on their way to adapting to the harsh realities of the modern world. Ideally, they will be successful in their endeavor, so that we do not lose the contribution of these people who, in the words of Secretary of State Seward, are gifted, vigorous, and energetic.

MOVING ON

We have explored the customs, history, and current situations today of five major groups of endangered peoples in the world. There are numerous others—some nomadic, like those mentioned in this book; others fairly settled, such as the many recently contacted tribes in the New Guinea highlands. In our own country, daily newspapers often print articles about the many native Americans who are caught between two worlds, that of mainstream society and that of their own natal group.

Today, as always, we are at a crossroads. Behind us are all the mistakes we've made as "outsiders" and the lessons we have learned. Ahead is an unsure future for tribal minorities. Judging from the past, it would seem that once contact is made with any tribal group in today's world the group needs both organizing from within and securing the support of outsiders. As you probably realize by now, even if the intentions of outsiders are honorable, their initial contact exposes any tribal group to diseases and trade items that are destined to change its very fabric of life forever. Then, too, tribal people by the fact of their difference and perceived inferiority from mainstream society continue to encounter prejudice and discrimination that fosters an array of serious problems. In some instances the group can cope; in others the problems are so severe that the group either totally assimilates into mainstream society or becomes extinct.

But the report from the tribal front is not all pessimistic. Outsiders are becoming more sensitive to the issues that indigenous peoples face. One leading indicator of this hopeful sign is seen in the increasing number of films that focus on the struggle of native Americans for their land and their heritage. Exposés by reporters on attempts by big business to exploit indigenous groups are helping to fuel the growing public awareness of the injustices in our global backyard. So, too, are briefings by environmentalists about how actions such as cutting down forests, building new hydroelectric plants, and mining newly discovered minerals affect the lands and living species around them.

On a local and regional level, a number of native groups are starting to organize in determined efforts to save or regain their homelands. One such group is the Kayapo of the Amazon River in Brazil, who were not contacted until 1965. After that time, gold miners, loggers, and ranchers tore down vast tracts of the forest and polluted the rivers. Their chief, Paulo Paiakan, has learned to speak Portuguese so that he can talk with government officials. He has also brought together Indians and members of the environmental movement to save

—139—

his people, and to remind everyone that by destroying the Amazon, people are destroying his tribe's environment as well as their own. He has helped to spread the word that rain forests are vital: because they absorb carbon dioxide and emit oxygen into the atmosphere, their destruction affects weather patterns and contributes to global warming and the greenhouse effect. Paiakan has traveled to the United States and other countries to give speeches about the growing urgency of his people's problem. When Brazilian President Fernando Collor de Mello set aside forestland for the Yanomami, he also approved some 19,000 square miles (49,210 sq km) to be set aside for the 4,000 Kayapo, now living in a dozen villages.

On a more international level, the United Nations, created after World War II in 1945, now provides indigenous peoples with the possibility of having an international forum where they can present their grievances. The Working Group on Indigenous Populations, founded in 1982 by the United Nations Commission on Human Rights, gathers information about the situation of indigenous peoples worldwide and recommends international laws to protect their rights.

But perhaps the most hopeful news of all is the growing international movement of indigenous peoples' organizations. These increasingly vocal groups, numbering several hundred by now, have mushroomed during the last decades. One of the most important is the World Council of Indigenous Peoples (WCIP). Founded in 1975, the WCIP serves as an umbrella group for indigenous organizations from all over the world. At a conference held in

Panama in 1984, the group resolved "to educate the world about the injustices done to them through international tribunals and fora, make more use of the media and increase and make more effective the alliances with other indigenous and non-indigenous peoples."

Public awareness has also been strengthened by the international controversy launched over the 1992 Christopher Columbus Quincentenary jubilee, marking the 500th anniversary of Christopher Columbus's arrival in the Americas. Those supporting the celebration hailed Columbus's courage, vision, and endurance. Those opposed—primarily American Indians, Hispanics, and blacks—claimed that Columbus should not be feted, since some 90 percent of the indigenous peoples he made contact with in 1492 were killed by European conquest and diseases. This controversy has helped us reexamine the past, the present, and the future. While we cannot undo yesterday, we can strive to be fairer and more humane today and tomorrow to everyone who shares our planet.

But no matter how fair and humane we are, we cannot stop change. As anthropologists are well aware, cultures never stay the same. Even if we only examine our own society or our own ethnic group, we realize that change is a constant in our lives. It would be naive to expect the Yanomami, the San, and any other tribal group to remain static in this age of Coke bottles falling from the sky and new technological advances transforming how we think as well as what we do. Furthermore, change in and of itself isn't inherently evil, unless change deprives people of what they hold most dear: their lives and those of their loved ones as well as their heritage and their homelands.

There is no doubt that all endangered peoples face difficult decisions and challenges in the years ahead. Regardless of how well organized they are, and how much outside support they receive, they must all still wrestle with the problem of how much to assimilate into mainstream society and how much to remain unique.

While the answer may be a very personal one to individuals within tribal groups, many anthropologists, scientists, and concerned outsiders are trying to help tribal people as best they can. They realize that taking away peoples' land and means of livelihood sets up a domino effect that results in a wealth of serious problems that include homelessness, malnutrition, alcoholism, violence, and suicide. Bearing the past in mind, concerned supporters urge that tribal people be granted equal status with other citizens of their country, and that their introduction to mainstream society is made gradually so that their identity and self-esteem remain strong.

Perhaps 1993, proclaimed by the United Nations as the Year of the Indigenous Peoples, will usher in a more universal awareness of the problems faced by today's indigenous populations. Yet, even as we ponder how to make amends for past mistakes while preventing new damage, the elders of many tribes voice the fear that we may be too late. These men and women watch with sad and knowing eyes as their grandchildren and great grandchildren face an increasing array of options and temptations from the modern world. The elders, who speak the language of nature and the spirit world, know that it is a "different world" now, yet they urge youngsters to not forget the richness of their culture and their connection with their past, their land, and the unseen spirit world.

Like the elders, many concerned anthropologists worry that even tribes able to physically survive today's dizzying pace of change are faced with cultural doom unless a concerted effort is made actively and philosophically to save them. Yet, unfortunately, it sometimes seems that officials are more willing to preserve the rights of endangered animals than of endangered peoples. Finally, aside from the basic humane reasons to care about our global neighbors, it seems short-sighted to ignore the fact that we are all connected: we destroy a little more of ourselves each time we destroy some segment of the human family. Our fragile planet depends upon our abilities to make the best use of every resource, from plants to people.

As life moves on, impassioned supporters will continue trying to help tribal groups honor their past while exposing their plight to the public, build strong internal and international organizations, and make use of the modern world's advances. Meanwhile, tribal elders will continue to keep their vigil. From the Kalahari Desert to the Amazon rain forest, these reservoirs of folklore silently wait, ready to be of service if only they are asked.

ORGANIZATIONS
— of —
INTEREST

If you want to find out more about endangered peoples, you may want to write to some of the groups below. Many publish magazines, newsletters, bulletins, and other materials of interest. Note that this is only a partial list of the hundreds of groups comprising indigenous/tribal peoples or with a special interest in helping indigenous/tribal peoples.

INTERNATIONAL ORGANIZATIONS

Anti-Slavery Society
180 Brixton Road
London SW9 6AT
United Kingdom

Committee for Indigenous Minority Research (CIMRA)
5 Caledonian Road
London N1
United Kingdom

Cultural Survival*
53-A Church Street
Cambridge
MA 02138
USA

Indigenous Peoples Network Research Center
PO Box 364
Rochester VT 05767
USA

International Work Group For Indigenous Affairs (IWGIA)
Fiolstraede 10
DK-1171 Copenhagen K
Denmark

Inuit Circumpolar Conference
650 32nd Ave.,
Suite 404
H8T 3K4 Lachine,
Quebec, Canada

* Of special interest because of the many publications they publish and distribute.

Survival International*
310 Edgware Road
London W2 IDY
United Kingdom

Third World Resource
  Center
125 Tecumseh Road
N8X 1E8 Windsor
Ottawa, Ontario
Canada

United Nations—Center
  For Human Rights
Palais de Nations
'Room D416
1211 Geneva 10
Switzerland

United Nations Working
  Group on Indigenous
  Populations
Center for Human Rights
Palais des Nations
Room D416
1211 Geneva 10
Switzerland

Workgroup for Indige-
  nous Peoples (WIP)
PO Box 4098
1009 AB Amsterdam
Netherlands

World Council of Indige-
  nous Peoples
(International Secretariat)
555 King Edward Avenue
Ottawa, Ontãrio
Canada KIN 6 NS

YANOMAMI

American Friends of
  Venezuelan Indians
  (AFVI)
c/o Dr. Napoleon Chagnon
Anthropology Department
University of California
  at Santa Barbara
Santa Barbara, CA
  93106
USA

South and Meso Ameri-
  can Indian
  Information Center
PO Box 7550
Oakland, CA 94707
USA

Yanomami Survival Fund
c/o Dr. Napoleon Chagnon
Anthropology Department
University of California
  at Santa Barbara
Santa Barbara, CA
  93106
USA

SAN/BUSHMEN

Kung/San Foundation
c/o Cultural Survival
11 Divinity Avenue
Cambridge, MA 02138
USA

BAMBUTI/AFRICAN PYGMIES

Ituri Fund
c/o Cultural Survival
11 Divinity Avenue
Cambridge, MA 02138
USA

AUSTRALIAN ABORIGINES

Aboriginal Mining Information Centre
PO Box 237
Healesville 3777
Victoria
Australia

Anthropology Resource Center
PO Box 15266
Washington DC
20003-0266
USA

Institute For Aboriginal Development
PO Box 2531
0870 Alice Springs, N.T.
Australia

National Federation of Land Councils
PO Box 3620
Alice Springs
N.T. 5750
Australia

National Organization of Aboriginal and Islander Legal Services
PO Box 143
Chippendale 2008
N.S.W. Australia

INUITS (ESKIMOS)

Committee for Original Peoples Entitlement (COPE)
Box 2000
Innuvik, N.W.T.
Canada

Inuit Tapirisat of Canada
176 Gloucester St. (3rd Floor)
Ottawa, Ontario
Canada

—146—

SOURCE NOTES

INTRODUCTION

(1) Clay, Jason. "Yahgan and Ona—The Road to Extinction." *Cultural Survival*, Fall 1984, pp. 5–8.

YANOMAMI

(1) Brooke, James. "Brazilian Agency to Destroy Jungle Airstrips." *New York Times*, September 18, 1990, sec. B, p. 6.

(2) Brooke, James. "In an Almost Untouched Jungle, Gold Miners Threaten Indian Ways." *New York Times*, September 18, 1990, sec. B, pp. 5–6.

(3) Brooke, James. "Venezuela Befriends Tribe, but What's Venezuela?" *New York Times*, September 11, 1991, sec. A, p. 8.

(4) Golden, Tom. "Talk about Culture Shock: Ant People in Sky-high Huts." *New York Times*, April 17, 1991, sec. B, pp. 1, 4.

SAN/BUSHMEN OF THE KALAHARI DESERT

(1) Yellen, John E. "The Transformation of the Kalahari !Kung." *Scientific American*, April 1990, pp. 96–105.

(2) Drucker, Elizabeth, "The Gods Must Be Crazy II, Jamie Uys—From Botswana to the Big Screen." *American Film* v. 15, October 1989, p. 97.

—147—

BAMBUTI/PYGMIES OF THE ITURI FOREST

(1) Shreeve, James. "Madam, I'm Adam." *Discover,* June 1991, p. 24.

(2) Bailey, Robert. "The Efe Archers of the African Rain Forest." *National Geographic,* November 1989, pp. 664–686.

(3) Wilkie, David S. and Morelli, Gilda A. "Coming of Age in the Ituri." *Natural History,* October 1991, pp. 55–62.

(4) Hart, John A. and Teresa B. "The Mbuti of Zaire." *Cultural Survival,* Fall 1984, pp. 18–20.

ABORIGINES OF AUSTRALIA

(1) Howse, John. "Lost in a Land of Plenty." *Macleans,* p. 48.

(2) Hughes, Robert. "Evoking the Spirit Ancestors." *Time,* October 31, 1988, pp. 79–80.

(3) Wright, Belinda and Breeden, Stanley. "The First Australians." *National Geographic,* February 1988, p. 278.

INUITS (ESKIMOS)

(1) Tombs, George. "Canada's New Arctic." *World Monitor,* July 1990, pp. 40–48.

(2) Tritt, Lincoln. "Notes from Arctic Village." *Alaska Magazine,* August 1991, p. 34.

(3) "Village Rights." *The Economist,* August 12, 1989, p. 24.

GLOSSARY

GENERAL
Assimilation. The process of absorbing a culturally distinct group into the prevailing or mainstream society.

Indigenous. Native to an area.

Mainstream. The prevalent or most influential society in a group.

YANOMAMI
Curare. Poison made from a wild jungle vine.

Garimpeiros. Gold seekers in Amazon.

Hekuri. Yanomami word for spirit.

Shabano. Thatched-roof communal village, consisting of houses made from palm leaves and arranged in a circular pattern.

SAN/BUSHMEN
Eland. Large antelope which the San painted in many pictures.

Gaua. Spirit of the dead.

Kaross. Leather cape made from animal hide and usually belted at the waist with a sinew cord and knotted at the shoulder.

Scherm. Little huts of the San.

Ur/Um. Supernatural power.

Werf. San village.

BAMBUTI/AFRICAN PYGMIES

Elima. A Bambuti girl's coming of age ritual.

Molimo. Festival performed to wake up the sleeping forest.

Nkumba. A Bambuti boy's coming of age ceremony, dutifully held to appease the village, although not recognized by the tribes.

ABORIGINES OF AUSTRALIA

Boomerang. Flat, curved wooden object that either returns or does not return to thrower.

Coolamons. Curved containers made out of bark or wood.

Corroborees. Ceremonies filled with songs, dances, and storytelling.

Dreamtime. When all things were created.

Moiety. Division of a tribe into halves.

Tucker. Aboriginal word for food.

Uluru. Known as Ayers Rock to non-Aborigines, this is the Aborigines' most sacred site.

Woomeras. Wooden spear throwers.

INUITS

Angakkoq. Shaman or medicine person.

Caribou. Wild North American reindeer.

Harpoon. Spear with a detachable head.

Igloo. A word from the Inuit word *iglu*, which was used for all houses.

Kayak. Usually a one-man boat with a wooden or bone frame covered with sealskin.

Leister spear. A special spear with prongs on either side and another in the center.

Shaman. Person with ability to contact spirits and foretell the future.

Umiak. A boat larger than a kayak and used to hunt larger sea animals.

BIBLIOGRAPHY

BOOKS

Berger, Julian. *Report from the Frontier: The State of the World's Indigenous Peoples*. Cambridge, Mass.: Zed Books Ltd., London Cultural Survival Inc., 1987.

Blainey, Geoffrey. *Triumph of the Nomads: A History of Aboriginal Australia*. New York: The Overlook Press, 1976.

Brain, Robert. *The Last Primitive Peoples*. New York: Crown Publishers, 1976.

Bruemmer, Fred. *The Arctic World*. San Francisco, Calif.: Key Porter Books Limited, 1985.

Burch, Ernest S. Jr. *The Eskimos*. Norman: University of Oklahoma Press, 1988.

Chagnon, Napoleon A. *Yanomamo: The Fierce People*. New York: Holt, Rinehart and Winston, 1977 Second Edition.

DeVore, Irven and Lee, Richard B., eds. *Man the Hunter*. Chicago: Aldine Publishing Company, 1968.

Good, Kenneth with David Chanoff. *Into the Heart*. New York: Simon & Schuster, 1991.

Hirschfelder, Arlene. *Happily May I Walk: American Indians and Alaska Natives Today*. New York: Charles Scribner's Sons, 1986.

Lizot, Jacques. *Tales of the Yanomami*. London: Cambridge University Press, 1976.

Luling, Virginia. *Aborigines*. London: Macdonald Educational, 1979.

MacDougall, Trudie. *Beyond Dreamtime: The Life and Lore of the Aboriginal Australian*. New York: Coward, McCann & Geoghegan, 1978.

Reader, John. *Man on Earth*. Austin: University of Texas Press, 1988.

Reyburn, Bruce. "The Forgotten Struggle of Australia's Aboriginal People." *Cultural Survival Quarterly* 12 (3) p. 7–10.

Smith, Greg J. H. *Eskimos: The Inuit of the Arctic*. Vero Beach, Fl.: Rourke Publications, 1987.

Terrill, Ross. *The Australians*. New York: Simon & Schuster, 1987.

Thomas, Elizabeth Marshall. *The Harmless People*. New York: Alfred A. Knopf, 1968.

Turnbull, Colin M. *The Forest People*. New York: Simon & Schuster, 1961.

Van Der Post, Laurens, and Taylor, Jane. *Testament to the Bushmen*. New York: Viking, 1984.

Weyer, Edward Jr. *Primitive People Today*. Garden City, N.Y.: Doubleday & Company, 1961.

PERIODICALS

Bailey, Robert C. "The Efe: Archers of the African Rain Forest." *National Geographic*, November 1989, pp. 664–689.

Bailey, Robert C., and Devore, I. "Research on the Efe and Lese Populations of the Ituri Forest, Zaire." *American Journal of Physical Anthropology*, April 1989, pp. 459–472.

Brooke, James. "In an Almost Untouched Jungle, Gold Miners Threaten Indian Ways." *New York Times*, September 18, 1990, sec. B, pp. 5–6.

Clay, Jason, ed. "Organizing to Survive." *Cultural Survival Quarterly*, Fall 1984.

Condon, Richard G., and Stern, Pamela R. "Uluhaktokmiut and Economic Change." *Cultural Survival Quarterly*, Fall 1984, pp. 38–40.

Drucker, Elizabeth. "The Gods Must Be Crazy II, Jamie Uys—From Botswana to the Big Screen." *American Film*, v. 15, October 1989, p. 97.

Golden, Tim, "Talk about Culture Shock: Ant People in Sky-High Huts." *New York Times*, April 17, 1991, sec. B, pp. 1, 4.

Hart, John A., and Hart, Terese B. "The Mbuti of Zaire." *Cultural Survival Quarterly*, Fall 1984, pp. 18–20.

Headland, Thomas N. "Hunter-Gatherers and Their Neighbors from Prehistory to the Present." *Current Anthropology*, February 1989, pp. 43–67.

Howse, John. "Lost in a Land of Plenty." *Macleans*, May 2, 1988, p. 48.

Hughes, Robert. "Evoking the Spirit Ancestors." *Time*, October 31, 1988, pp. 79–80.

Marshall, John. "Death Blow to the Bushmen." *Cultural Survival Quarterly*, Fall 1984, pp. 13–17.

Reiss, Spencer. "The Last Days of Eden." *Newsweek*, December 3, 1990, pp. 48–50.

Ritchie, Claire. "Update on the Status of Bushmanland." *Cultural Survival Quarterly*, Fall 1988, pp. 34–35.

Shreeve, James. "Madam, I'm Adam." *Discover*, June 1991, p. 24.

Smith, Eric Alden. "Inuit of the Canadian Eastern Arctic." *Cultural Survival Quarterly*, Fall 1984, pp. 32–37.

Sturgis, Kent. "The Twilight People." *Alaska*, January 1989, pp. 22–25/53–56.

Tombs, George. "Canada's New Arctic." *World Monitor*, July 1990, pp. 42–48.

Tritt, Lincoln. "Notes from Arctic Village." *Alaska Magazine*, August 1991, p. 34.

Volkman, Toby Alice. "The San in Transition." *Documentary Educational Resources (D.E.R.) and Cultural Survival*, November 1982.

Wilford, John Nobel. "Discovering Columbus." *New York Times Magazine*, August 11, 1991, pp. 25–28/45–49/55.

Wilkie, David S., and Morelli, Gilda A. "Pitfalls of the Pygmy Hunt." *Natural History*, December 1988, pp. 33–40.

Wright, Belinda, and Breeden, Stanley. "The First Australians." *National Geographic*, February 1988, pp. 278–292.

WuDunn, Sheryl. "Original Australians: Life in 2 Worlds." *New York Times*, Oct. 2, 1990, p. A4.

Yellen, John E. "The Transformation of the Kalahari !Kung." *Scientific American*, April 1990, pp. 96–105.

Zich, Arthur. "Botswana the Adopted Land." *National Geographic*, December 1990, pp. 71–96.

"Collor Revokes Decrees Trimming Indian Land." *The Tucson Citizen*, April 21, 1990, p. 10.

"Hordes of Disease-Spreading Prospectors Invade New Indian Lands." *Arizona Daily Star*, November 25, 1990, C-2.

"Village Rights." *The Economist*, August 12, 1989, p. 24.

FOR FURTHER READING

BOOKS

Berger, Julian. *Report from the Frontier: The State of the World's Indigenous Peoples*. Cambridge, Mass.: Zed Books Ltd., London Cultural Survival Inc., 1987.

Blainey, Geoffrey. *Triumph of the Nomads: A History of Aboriginal Australia*. New York: The Overlook Press, 1976.

Brain, Robert. *The Last Primitive Peoples*. New York: Crown Publishers, 1976.

Burch, Ernest S., Jr. *The Eskimos*. Norman: University of Oklahoma Press, 1988.

Chagnon, Napoleon A. *Yanomamo: The Fierce People*. Second Edition. New York: Holt, Rinehart and Winston, 1977.

DeVore, Irven, and Lee, Richard B., ed. *Man the Hunter*. Chicago: Aldine Publishing Company, 1968.

Good, Kenneth, with David Chanoff. *Into the Heart*. New York: Simon & Schuster, 1991.

Hirschfelder, Arlene. *Happily May I Walk: American Indians and Alaska Natives Today*. New York: Charles Scribner's Sons, 1986.

Luling, Virginia. *Aborigines*. London: Macdonald Educational, 1979.

MacDougall, Trudie. *Beyond Dreamtime: The Life and Lore of the Aboriginal Australian*. New York: Coward, McCann & Geoghegan, 1978.

Reader, John. *Man on Earth*. Austin: University of Texas Press, 1988.

Smith, Greg J. H. *Eskimos: The Inuit of the Arctic*. Vero Beach, Fl.: Rourke Publications, 1987.

Thomas, Elizabeth Marshall. *The Harmless People*. New York: Alfred A. Knopf, 1968.

Turnbull, Colin M. *The Forest People*. New York: Simon & Schuster, 1961.

Van Der Post, Laurens, and Taylor, Jane. *Testament to the Bushmen*. New York: Viking, 1984.

PERIODICALS

Cultural Survival Quarterly
Cultural Survival
11 Divinity Avenue
Cambridge
MA 02136
USA

Although many of the organizations listed earlier in this book publish materials, the *Cultural Survival Quarterly* is outstanding in its field. Many anthropologists have referred me to it as being in depth, up-to-date, and understandable by nonanthropologists. You may want to write to Cultural Survival for a list of subjects covered in previous quarterlies and a list of other publications that they distribute.

FILMS
DOCUMENTARY EDUCATIONAL RESOURCES
(DER)
101 Morse Street
Watertown, Massachusetts 02172
Telephone (617) 926-0491
Fax (617) 926-9519

DER produces and distributes many films about endangered peoples, including the !Kung San/ Bushmen, the Yanomami, and the Inuit (Eskimo). It is a very valuable resource—the company's catalog of available films reads like a book on endangered peoples.

INDEX

Aborigines, 10
  culture, 81–97
  current situation,
    99–104
  history, 80–81, 88–
    90, 97–99
Aka, 67
Alaska, 106, 108, 113,
  127, 132–136
Alaska, Federation of
  Natives, 134
American Friends of
  Venezuelan Indians,
  33
Angola, 40, 52, 56
Assimilation, problems
  of, 9, 27–29, 32–
  33, 53–56, 75–79,
  101, 128, 131–132,
  135–136, 138–
  139
Australia, 80–81

Bailey, Robert, 78–
  79
Bambuti, 10

culture, 60–74
  current situation,
    74–79
  history, 59–60
Bantu, 39, 61, 73, 76,
  77–78
Botswana, 40, 41, 52,
  55–56
Brazil, 13, 14, 27–32,
  139–140
Bushmen. See San

Canada, 106, 108,
  131–132, 136
Central African
  Republic, 59
Chagnon, Napoleon,
  13, 19–20, 21, 27,
  30, 33
Christopher Columbus
  Quincentenary, 141
Collor de Mello,
  Fernando, 29, 140
Committee for Original
  People's Entitlement,
  132

— 158 —

Cook, James, 98
Cultural extinction, 7,
9–10

Denmark, 130–131
Diseases, imported, 9,
27, 28, 128, 130, 138
Dobi !Kung San, 53–54

Efe, 63, 67, 77, 78
Eskimos. *See* Inuit

*Gods Must Be Crazy,
The*, 34, 35, 58
Good, Kenneth, 21
Greenland, 106, 108,
111, 127, 129, 130–
131, 136

Habitat, destruction of,
9, 13, 27–29, 41,
52–53, 55–56, 75–
77, 78–79, 98–101,
128–129, 131, 133,
134, 138–140
Harmless People, The
(Thomas), 52
Homer, 60
Hottentot, 37, 39

Iliad (Homer), 60
International Whaling
Commission, 134
Into the Heart (Good), 21
Inuit, 10

culture, 108–127
current situation,
129–137
history, 106–108,
127–129
Inuit Circumpolar
Conference, 136–137
Inuit Tapirisat of
Canada, 132
Ituri Fund, 79

Jansz, Willem, 97

Kakadu National Park,
100–101
Kayapo, 139
Kopenawa, Davi, 32– 33
!Kung San, 35, 53–54
!Kung San Foundation,
57

Lese, 63, 77, 78
Lucotte, Gerard, 59

Marshall, John, 34–35,
57–58
Mbuti, 67, 72

Namibia, 40, 52, 56–57
New York Times, 32
N!Xau, 34–35

Onas. *See* Selk'nam

Paiakan, Paulo, 139– 140

Perez, Carlos Andres, 30
Phillip, Arthur, 80
Physical extinction, 7,
  9, 11–12
Preservation of
  endangered cultures,
  10, 11, 29–32, 33,
  57–58, 79, 100–104,
  130–131, 132, 134,
  136–137, 139–143
Pygmies. *See* Bambuti

San, 10, 34
  culture, 35–37, 40,
    42–43, 44–52
  current situation,
    41–42, 43–44,
    52–58
  history, 37–40, 41,
    44, 52
Selk'nam, 11–12
Seward, William H.,
  105
Siberia, 106, 129–130
Simba Rebellion, 75–76
South Africa, 40, 52, 56
Sua, 67

Tasmania, 81, 99
Thomas, Elizabeth, 52
Truganini, 99
Turnbull, Colin, 74

Uluru National Park, 100

United Nations, 140
Uys, Jaime, 34, 58

Venezuela, 13, 21, 30,
  31, 33
Von Humbolt, Baron,
  15

Working Group on
  Indigenous
  Populations, 140
World Bank, 78
World Council of
  Indigenous Peoples,
  140–141
World War II, 133
World Wildlife Fund, 78

Yanomami, 10
  culture, 13–27
  current situation,
    27–33, 140
  history, 15
Yanomami Survival
  Fund, 33
*Yanomamo: The Fierce
  People* (Chagnon), 20
Yenguyam, Aram, 87–
  88

Zaire, 60
Zambia, 52
Zimbabwe, 52